# Chelsea couldn't shake the feeling of disorientation

"The statement is just normal police procedure," the handsome doctor reassured her. "You'll have to give them the usual. Name—"

A total blankness enveloped her.

"Age—"

She should know this. It shouldn't take a rocket scientist to know when she was born.

"Address—"

She tried to picture home, and all she drew was emptiness. She couldn't remember the basics! Seized with a terror so strong her entire body shook, she bit her tongue, and the coppery taste of blood flooded her mouth. Unshed tears gripped her throat and squeezed so tight she couldn't draw breath.

She didn't know who she was. Or where she lived. Or what she did for a living. She couldn't remember anything before the moment she woke in this bed.

Dear Reader,

Imagine waking up in a hospital with no memory and with a tiny infant in your arms—a baby you've never seen before!

So begins *A Baby To Love* by Susan Kearney. It's the third and final book in the LOST & FOUND trilogy, started by Dani Sinclair and Kelsey Roberts.

We hope you've enjoyed all three LOST & FOUND books!

Regards,

Debra Matteucci
Senior Editor & Editorial Coordinator
Harlequin Books
300 East 42nd Street
New York, NY 10017

# A Baby To Love
## Susan Kearney

## *Harlequin Books*

TORONTO • NEW YORK • LONDON
AMSTERDAM • PARIS • SYDNEY • HAMBURG
STOCKHOLM • ATHENS • TOKYO • MILAN
MADRID • WARSAW • BUDAPEST • AUCKLAND

ISBN 0-373-22378-1

A BABY TO LOVE

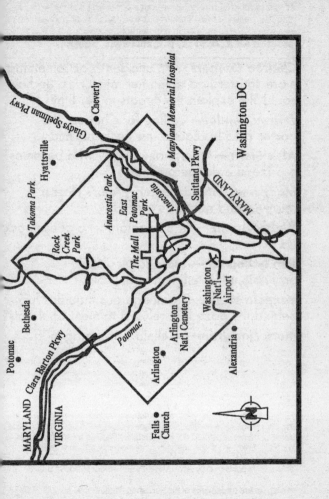

# CAST OF CHARACTERS

*Chelsea Connors*—An accident...or something more sinister had stolen her memories. So how could she explain the threats to her life?

*Jeffrey Kendall*—Falling for Chelsea, the doctor risks his career, his neck, his heart.

*Alex Stern*—An orphaned baby who becomes a prize in a dangerous game.

*Mary and Tom Carpenter*—Alex's closest relatives and not to be trusted.

*Walter Brund*—An accountant who doesn't add up.

*Sandy Ronald*—A terrific secretary—professional, intelligent and...cold.

*Vanessa Wells*—Did dangerous thoughts lurk behind the gaze that refused to meet Chelsea's?

*Mark Lindstrom*—A client with an agenda.

# Prologue

*Perfect. She's falling right into my trap.*

From deep in the bushes, hands parted branches to reveal approaching prey. Chelsea Connors tossed dark hair over her shoulder, stepped out of her car and crossed the narrow street, the midday sun glinting off the clasp of her leather purse.

*That's it, keep walking.*

Striding forward, her sensible two-inch heels tapping boundless self-confidence, she slipped through the gap in the fence and into the split-level house's weed-choked yard. She proceeded without looking right or left, as if it would never occur to her that exposing her back left her vulnerable.

Next door a dog, senses keen, yapped. Barking as if to warn her of imminent danger, the animal tore back and forth, rattling the chain that tethered it to a spike in the ground. She ignored the warning and advanced another two paces toward the porch stairs, seemingly oblivious to the stealth of footsteps behind her.

The dog's frenzy swelled to a howl. Chelsea turned, her foot on the second step.

Spotting the baton swinging toward her head, her eyes flared in panic. ''Don't!''

Belatedly she lifted a hand to protect herself.

*A futile gesture.*

The baton slammed into her skull, and she spun. With a whimpering cry, she crumpled down the steps onto the patchy lawn in a heap.

The attacker snatched her purse from her shoulder, then raised the baton to finish her off.

*Perfect.*

# Chapter One

An incessant beeping tweaked her consciousness, and the acrid scent of antiseptic stung her nostrils. She fluttered her eyelids, then winced at the too-bright fluorescent lights that aggravated the throbbing in her head.

"Welcome back."

Her perceptions sharpened at the resonant tone of the masculine voice. Without moving her aching head, she glanced sideways to spy the owner of that splendid voice hovering over her bed. He fingered his stethoscope while sexy eyes as blue as his rumpled scrubs appraised her with professional thoroughness. She'd never seen eyes that particular shade of teal before. At least, she didn't think she had. With a frown that shot pain from her jaw to the back of her head, she realized she couldn't remember.

The doctor didn't seem familiar. Although if she had to awaken groggy, dizzy and in pain, with her head pounding like a jackhammer, she couldn't have asked for someone better to look at.

He appeared about twenty-seven or -eight, just over six feet tall and slender. He wore his black hair cropped short. Even without a smile, his face was compellingly handsome. When he grinned, only a rugged jawline kept his high cheekbones, straight nose and full lips from model-prettiness.

She dwelled on his patrician looks instead of occupying her thoughts with other issues—like what had happened to her and how she'd ended up here. For that matter, she didn't know where *here* was. Her gaze darted about the hospital room. An IV was taped to her hand. Wires from the beeping heart monitor disappeared under her gown, attached to her chest with sticky pads.

"Where am I?" Her voice was unrecognizable to her ears, no doubt due to her dry throat.

"Maryland Memorial Hospital. I'm Dr. Jeffrey Kendall," he introduced himself in that husky tone she couldn't help liking. "You suffered a trauma to the head. We've already done a CAT scan of your brain." Before she could ask, he explained. "It's like an X ray. And the EEG recorded your brain waves to check for abnormalities."

How long had she been here? A glance at the clock radio beside the bed told her it was just after 3:00 p.m. But the time held no meaning for her. And why couldn't she recall the examinations? Afraid to ask, she tensed her shoulders, which magnified the pounding in her head.

Perhaps she'd still been asleep when they'd run the tests, and the results weren't yet back. That must be it. She ran a shaking hand across a creased brow grown slick with nervous perspiration.

"Relax, this won't hurt a bit." Dr. Kendall's mouth quirked upward, his teasing a balm to her raw nerves. With the caring hands of a physician, the nails clipped close and immaculately clean, he plucked a penlight from his pocket and shined it into her pupils. "Look straight ahead, please."

A minute later, he ordered, "Now watch my finger."

As he traced the air, she followed his movements.

"Very good." He slipped the penlight back into his pocket, reached for the stethoscope around his neck and paused. "Hey, no need to look so worried. Except for the knot on your head, there doesn't seem to be anything wrong with you."

She groaned and massaged her temples. "My head hurts."

"Sorry. Patients with head injuries aren't allowed painkillers." He listened to her heart, then checked her pulse.

The doctor didn't seem inclined to chat, but she needed answers. "How'd I get here?"

Dr. Kendall consulted his chart, but she suspected it was more to avoid her gaze while revealing bad news than from his need to recall information. "EMS brought you in."

That explained how she'd arrived but not why. He was holding back; she knew it. "What's wrong with my head?"

His blue eyes radiated sympathy, and for a moment she feared he was going to deliver some horrible prognosis. "A small cut. Nothing to worry about. We were hoping you could tell us what happened."

His words took her by surprise. She didn't remember a thing. A twinge of fear tightened her stomach. *Don't panic. There could be a rational explanation.* Maybe she'd been in a car accident.

"I promised to have a nurse call the cops when you woke to give a statement. Do you feel up to it?"

"Why do the police need a statement?"

"To complete their report. They were on the scene after you were found."

"I don't remember."

"That's not unusual. EMS brought you in, and we did the tests. You woke up the first time about a half hour ago and you couldn't tell us what happened."

"I couldn't?" She sensed he was filtering information, weighing his words to avoid telling her something unpleasant. Every muscle in her body tensed. What didn't he want to tell her?

"The nurse called the cops then, and I believe an officer is waiting down the hall."

She couldn't shake the disorientation akin to awakening from a sound sleep, but that was a feeling that didn't last this long. It was as if the incidents he'd described had happened to someone else—not her. It seemed odd that she couldn't recall one detail of the experience, and the knots in her stomach twisted.

"The statement is just police procedure," he reassured her. "You'll have to give them the usual."

"The usual?"

"Name..."

A total blankness enveloped her.

"Age..."

She should know this. It shouldn't take a rocket scientist to know when she was born. She raised her hand and rubbed her pounding brow.

"Address..."

She tried to picture home, and all she drew was emptiness. Sweat beaded her lip.

"Witnesses, if any. That sort of thing."

His piercing blue eyes seemed to register her confusion. Her mind was like pages in a book written with disappearing ink. She didn't remember the trip to the hospital, her tests, waking up. Her memory bank was as desolate and empty as this cold hospital room. The fine hairs on her neck bristled. She couldn't recall the accident that had sent her here.

Her name? Her age? Her phone number? Oh, God! She couldn't remember the basics. Seized with a terror so strong her entire body shook, she bit her tongue, and the coppery taste of blood flooded her mouth. Tears welled in a throat closed so tight she couldn't draw breath.

The heart monitor beeped erratically. Dr. Kendall looked at her, concern filling his eyes. He reached for her hand. "Take it easy. Memory loss is common after a bump on the head."

As if balanced precariously on the lip of a precipice, with only his fingers to prevent a fatal fall, she clutched his hand. Horror rose like bile in her throat.

She didn't know who she was. Or where she lived. Or what she did for a living. She couldn't remember anything before the moment she'd woken in this bed.

*Don't panic. Don't panic. Don't panic.*

Had she completely lost her marbles? This didn't look like a psycho ward, but then she'd never been in one before. At least, she didn't think so. But then, for all she remembered, she might have lived here for years. And every day she woke up unable to recall the day before. She shuddered.

No, that wasn't right. Terror slammed into her, overwhelming her reasoning. She clenched his hand to calm blooming hysteria. When her head stopped hurting, she would remember.

*No need to panic. Be calm. Breathe.*

Taking a ragged breath, she caught sight of her frightened face in the polished metal surface of her bed tray. The green-eyed brunette staring back appeared comfortably familiar. She knew exactly how to twist her hair in a French braid to make the most of her high cheekbones. She could choose the lipstick color that would enhance her generous mouth. She recognized the tiny scar by her eyebrow, but how she'd obtained the injury, she couldn't say.

"I can't remember my name." To her relief, the words came out calmly, like a pilot sending a last message to air-traffic control before going down in an inevitable crash.

"Tell me what you can." Dr. Kendall spoke slowly, as if she were a child, his thumb massaging her wrist in a comforting way. Or maybe he was monitoring her pulse. No matter his reason, she appreciated his gesture.

"I remember the beep of the heart monitor, opening my eyes, seeing you."

"Nothing before that?"

She shook her head, unable to answer. Fresh fear invaded her body, a frigid stream of icy fluid sluicing through her veins. "I don't seem to have childhood memories, recollections of relatives or friends. Not so much as a memory of a family dog."

She shivered. She felt so alone, as if Dr. Kendall's warm hand were her only link to humanity. And she didn't want to fall apart in front of him.

Concentrating on his face, she made a conscious effort to collect herself. Their gazes locked, and for a moment she took solace in his simple empathy and kindly tone.

"There are two forms of amnesia," he said. "One is psychological, the other physical."

She gingerly lifted her hand to the knot on her head, fingering the bandage. "Surely I'm not crazy?"

"Most likely your injury caused the memory loss. Even if the amnesia is psychological, we wouldn't consider you insane."

"Really? You don't think it odd I can't even remember my name, and yet I'm dying for my favorite rocky-road ice cream with gobs of hot fudge and four maraschino cherries?"

"You remember that?"

"Apparently my taste buds don't have amnesia."

He chuckled at her sarcasm. "You seem to have a healthy sense of humor."

"Knowing what I do for a living might be more useful."

"There are two other possibilities here."

"What?"

"You may simply have fallen and bumped your head."

"Or?"

"We can't discount the possibility that you saw something you couldn't cope with, something your mind needed to escape from."

She couldn't recall much about her life, but his ominous words jarred her to her core. Her brain might have shut down due to a menacing or terrifying experience—something so horrible that her mind refused to deal with it.

"What happened to me?" she asked shakily.

"A neighbor found you alone and fully dressed at the bottom of a front stoop." He released her hand and stuck her chart under his arm. "Before we discuss this further, I think you should speak to the officer." He leaned toward a small cabinet and picked up a scuffed leather purse. "The police found this in the bushes one block away. The cash and credit cards are gone, but I believe your driver's license is intact."

She hesitated to take the unfamiliar purse from him, yet she couldn't prevent hope from blossoming. Was it really hers? When he continued to offer it to her, she accepted the bag, then clutched it to her chest like a security blanket.

She fingered the bag without opening it. "Why didn't you tell me my name?"

"We suspected you had amnesia the first time you awakened. You couldn't remember your name then, either." He spoke gently, compassion radiating from his eyes.

"Tell me my name, please."

"Unless you remember by yourself, your name will mean nothing to you."

She closed her eyes in exhaustion. "I guess I could get used to Jane Doe."

"Your name is Chelsea. Chelsea Connors."

Her lids popped open. "Chelsea Connors," she repeated, hoping the repetition would snake into her memory and unplug the hole into which her past had vanished. But the words were empty, echoing in her mind without meaning, merely vibrating in her thoughts before vanishing without a trace.

Her name brought no emotions, no revelations, no sudden understanding. Exactly what he'd warned her to expect. So why was she so disappointed?

"Don't try to force the memories. They'll return when you're ready."

*I'm ready now,* she wanted to scream. Instead, she hugged her purse, her only solid link to her past. She should tear open the metal clasp and look inside.

Dr. Kendall checked her IV and turned the volume of the heart monitor down. While he penned a few notations on her chart, she stared at the ceiling, her fingers tracing the pliable leather of her handbag.

He'd mentioned identification inside the purse. But would the contents reveal what kind of person she was? Whether she was a wise or a foolish woman? Giving or demanding? Strong or weak?

Although afraid of what she might find inside her bag, she refused to succumb to her fears. Working up her courage, she examined the supple leather, obviously expensive, the scratched but sturdy clasp and the broken shoulder strap. A purse like this wasn't cheap. Had she splurged to buy it? Had the purse been a gift from her mother? Or a lover?

The possibilities were endless. Recognizing her speculations as an excuse to stall, she fingered the clasp. Digging into a stranger's purse seemed too personal, a violation of privacy, even if that stranger was herself.

As if realizing she needed a moment to herself, Dr. Kendall clipped her chart to the foot of her bed and strode to the door. "I'll bring back the police officer. He might be enjoying his flirtation with the day nurse, but he must have better things to do."

She nodded as he left the room, her thoughts focused on the purse. *Open it.* It wasn't as if she had a lot to lose. Ignoring the increased rate of beeps that registered her trepidation, she yanked open the bag, turned it upside down and spilled the contents onto the sheet covering her lap.

A hairbrush. A compact. Two lipsticks. Keys. And a wallet.

Not so much, considering this was the sum of her life. Turning the purse upright, she opened it wide, ran her fingers along the inside to check for a zip pocket but found only a smooth silk lining.

She pulled her hand out and felt an oily residue on her fingertips. Rubbing her thumb against the slick pads of her fingers, she examined the interior of the empty purse. An amber stain, a tad larger than her hand, discolored the lining.

Unable to identify the curious stain that smelled like bananas, she set the bag aside and wiped her fingers clean on a tissue. To put off the inevitable search of her wallet, she snapped open the compact and grimaced at her appearance. Taking care not to dislodge the bandage on her head, she ran the brush through her hair as best she could, powdered her nose and applied lipstick. The normal, everyday motions came naturally, and yet she could not ever recall having done them before.

With a sigh, she replaced the brush and cosmetics in her purse and stared at the wallet, whose soft leather matched her purse. The wallet enticed her like Pandora's box with all its secrets and possible clues to her identity, to the kind of person she was. And like Pandora, once she explored the wallet's contents, she could never go back. But what if the information threw her another bad curve?

She had to shake off her foolishness. What could possibly be in there that she didn't want to see?

Gathering her courage, she checked the change purse, slots to hold credit cards, cash and a checkbook. She didn't have a dollar, a penny, a check.

Her driver's license was there with her address—a find. She'd just celebrated her twenty-eighth birthday last month. Although she didn't recognize the street name, at least she belonged somewhere. Quickly she thumbed through miscellaneous cards; attorney, health insurance, car insurance, check-cashing cards from the grocery store.

A receipt for a gun.

She jerked and the paper fluttered from numb fingers. A weapon? Forcing herself to look, but unwilling to touch the paper as if it could contaminate her, she checked the date. She'd purchased it within the past three weeks.

Why?

Her body shook and fear invaded every pore. Instinctively she knew she hated guns. She didn't know how she knew, but she did.

Her accident might not have had anything to do with the gun. But she couldn't ignore any possibilities. Had she simply fallen and banged her head?

If only she could remember.

As she rested against her pillow, her shoulders drooped with exhaustion. Her head ached from her effort to recall why she had needed a weapon. Was someone after her? Had she been threatened?

Or was she trying to make something dramatic out of a simple fall? She yawned, her thoughts unclear. She needed sleep.

The door of her room opened. "Ms. Connors?"

With effort she forced open gritty eyes. Dr. Kendall had returned with a short, hefty, blond-haired man in a too-tight uniform. The stranger sighed, as if he wished he could be anywhere but here.

"I'm Officer Russo, ma'am." When she didn't reply, his Adam's apple bobbed in his thick neck. "The doc says you don't remember a thing."

"The doc's right." She wet her dry lips with the tip of her tongue. Her heart seemed to thump erratically, but the beep of the heart monitor said otherwise.

Attentive to her needs, Dr. Kendall poured a glass of water, inserted a straw, then held it while she sipped. "Better?"

His acute powers of perception made him a wonderful doctor. The cool liquid eased the dryness in her parched throat. She lay back, grateful for small comforts, and thought how good it was to have him take care of her. "Thanks."

The officer bit the end of his pen. "We found you at the bottom of some steps. A neighbor's dog stood over you, barking like hell. If the neighbor hadn't called the dog off..."

She shivered. "The dog attacked me?"

"Actually the animal had yanked the stake he'd been chained to out of the ground to get to you. It seemed to be protecting you."

"From what?" She cocked her head. "Did the neighbor see anything?"

"Nope. That's why I wanted to talk to you."

"I'm afraid I'm not going to be much help. Where was I found?"

The officer glanced down to his pad. "At 75 Parkwood Drive. That's in Greybourne. By the way, your car is still parked there. We've been unable to determine if you slipped and fell or whether you were mugged."

Chelsea's eyes widened. "What was I doing there?"

"We don't know. The neighbors were unable to identify you."

Dr. Kendall's blue eyes looked askance. "Who was she going to see? Who lived at that address?"

"The house is a rental property and currently vacant."

"Maybe I was going to lease it," Chelsea suggested.

Dr. Kendall nodded. "That would make sense."

The officer put his pen in his front pocket with a sigh. "Ms. Connors lives in a much more expensive neighborhood. It's unlikely she would move to this area."

Chelsea shifted in the bed, drawing her knees toward her chest beneath the sheets. Speculation seemed useless, and the pounding in her head sharpened. "Well, maybe I was looking at the house for a friend."

"Or meeting someone. Do you know what happened to your gun, miss?"

"I don't even remember having a gun."

"By the smell of it, that's Hoppe's Number Nine gun oil in the lining of your purse, and you've got a receipt for a weapon."

Her head spun and she fought to concentrate on his words. "Was that a question?"

Dr. Kendall, an incredulous look on his face, turned to the officer. "What do you think she was doing with a gun?"

"Wait a minute," Chelsea interrupted. "Are you insinuating I'm some kind of criminal?"

The police officer shook his head. "Lady, I can't insinuate anything until you give me some answers."

"I'm sure there's a reasonable explanation for all this." Dr. Kendall shot the officer a warning look, and she couldn't decide whether to be pleased or annoyed by his attempt to protect her.

On second thought, after a glance at the doctor's dubious look, Chelsea reconsidered. Though the doctor sounded as if he were defending her, she suspected he had reservations but didn't want his patient upset. In a deliberate and soothing tone, Dr. Kendall continued. "As soon as her memory returns, Ms. Connors will tell you more."

Apparently realizing she couldn't help with the missing details, the patrolman closed his pad with a snap. "You ought to report the missing gun."

Frustration surged through her. "But I don't know that it *is* missing. I don't know if I had the gun with me or if that's an old stain."

"Is there reason to think that you didn't simply fall and bump your head? Did you have a fight with your husband?"

Chelsea held up her ringless left hand. "I don't think I'm married."

"Perhaps you had a lovers' quarrel?"

"I don't know. I can't remember." She worked hard to keep a whine from her voice.

Dr. Kendall spoke thoughtfully, "It seems odd that she wouldn't have any money at all, doesn't it? Even her change purse was cleaned out." The officer ignored her lack of funds. "If a crime is committed with your gun, your lack of memory is a convenient excuse."

"Not for me." She glared at the cop, decided it wasn't worth the trouble and closed her eyes to signal the end of the interview.

"She's obviously exhausted. And I think she's told you all she can. Perhaps you'd better go." Dr. Kendall straightened the sheet over her.

"Let me know if her memory returns." The door closed behind the officer.

Despite the drowsiness that floated like fog in her head, something the officer had said pricked her awake. "He said *if* my memory returns. Is there a chance I'll never remember?"

Dr. Kendall stepped to her side and gave her shoulder an encouraging pat. "It's possible but highly unlikely. Usually memory returns within a day or two."

He was keeping something from her. The room almost echoed with his unspoken qualifiers. "But?"

"It could be another day, a week or a month. I really can't say."

Beneath the covers, she dug her nails into her palms. "Why not?"

He checked the bandage on her head, gently lifting her hair from the injury. "Medicine is not an exact science. People heal at different rates. And there is still much we don't know about the human brain. Think of your memories as files stored in your head. The files may open piecemeal, and then your memory would return in stages. Or you may wake up tomorrow morning with full access to every file and be back to normal."

"Or the files could be permanently erased?"

"Oh, the files are there. It's just a matter of when you'll be able to read them."

Finished with his examination, he replaced the bandage. She relaxed under his gentle touch and wondered if all his patients received such care. The nurses probably adored him. His female patients would feel better just by looking at him.

Dr. Kendall turned up his lips in a most attractive smile. "The good news is that the hospital will release you tomorrow. Your EEG and CAT scans show no abnormalities."

"Let me get this straight. You're telling me there's nothing wrong with my brain except that it's lost a filing cabinet full of the last twenty-eight years of my life?"

He chuckled and his blue eyes danced. "Get some rest, Ms. Connors."

She lay back on her pillow, wearied with the hurdles she faced. From where would she summon the strength to find her place in the world? With her entire life a blank page, without memories of family or friends or lovers, haunting loneliness gnawed a hollow inside her.

"Wait. Suppose my family is looking for me?"

"Usually the family shows up within the first twenty-four hours."

She gasped. "How long have I been here?"

Dr. Kendall glanced at his watch. "Approximately thirty hours."

More than a day. Fighting back tears, she clenched and unclenched her fingers. *Calm down.* Perhaps not enough time had elapsed for anyone to notice her absence. Although she'd been gone overnight, perhaps she spoke to her parents only once a month, so there was no reason for them to feel concern. Perhaps she had a roommate who was accustomed to her spending a few days with a lover.

Without one person from her past to recognize her, she felt adrift. If she had a husband, surely he would have come for her. Loneliness gnawed at her. The hollow ache inside mushroomed until it encompassed her in a giant gray cloud of desolation. She could die in this hospital and no one might ever know—or care.

*So do something about it,* a little voice in the back of her consciousness urged.

Despite the fatigue weighing down her limbs like lead, she remained alert enough to watch Dr. Kendall reaching to open her door on his way out.

"Doctor, could you please bring me a phone?"

He sighed. "You should rest."

She'd pinned her chance of finding someone who knew her on a simple phone call and refused to back down now. "How can I, when I may have family wondering where I am? Let me make one phone call. Please."

As if understanding how vital making a connection to her past was to her sanity, he yielded. With a quick nod, he left, returning within minutes with a phone. After setting it on the bedside table and plugging it into the jack, he retreated to the far side of the room, giving her some privacy, but clearly unwilling to leave her alone.

Did he know how difficult this call would be? Did he expect hysterics if she didn't receive the answers she needed? If so, she vowed to disappoint him.

Unable to recall her phone number, Chelsea, with shaky hands, picked up the receiver and dialed directory assistance. Damn! Her number was unlisted. Now what?

A glance at the doctor revealed he wasn't about to allow her much more time. He stood against the wall, arms folded across his chest, leaning impatiently forward.

"Operator, this is an emergency. Would you please connect me to someone at . . ." She flipped open her wallet and gave her address.

"Hold, please."

Excited, Chelsea forced air into her lungs. She heard ringing. And ringing.

*Someone please pick up the phone. Talk to me. Tell me what I'm like.*

A recorder clicked on, and her taped voice greeted her. The operator disconnected after the first "Hello" and came back on the line. "I'm sorry, ma'am. There's no answer. Please try again later."

Disappointment chilled Chelsea, raising goose bumps on her arms. She couldn't control the shaking in her hands or the sudden chattering of her teeth. As she hung up the phone, discouraged, a tiny moan escaped her lips.

Could Dr. Kendall sense how close she was to screaming in frustration at her latest setback? If so, at least it kept him from abandoning her.

Within a moment, he neared her bed and took her cold hands into his large warm ones. She stiffened at his touch but then relaxed in the realization his gesture lacked sensuality. She squeezed his fingers like a frightened child seeking to connect to reality and banish an all-too-real nightmare. His caress was soothing. It felt so good to be touched, to allow his warmth to banish her chill.

She breathed in his male scent and took comfort in his strength. He remained still, holding her hands until the tightness left her shoulders and her breathing evened.

Minutes passed and the fearsome tension drained from her limbs. When she tipped her head back to thank him for his kindness and compassion, their gazes locked, igniting a different kind of tension.

He was just doing his job, she assured herself. No one could possibly be interested in a woman who couldn't even remember her name.

When she calmed, he eased his hands away. "You should rest," he stated in that voice she so adored, and she lay back on her pillow, willing to follow his suggestion.

At a sharp rap on the door, he turned, a small scowl flitting across his face at the disturbance.

A woman backed into the room, her wide hips clearing the doorway by mere inches. The newcomer was short, curly haired and in her middle fifties. Her booming voice matched her hefty size, no doubt waking patients throughout ICU.

The overweight woman turned and smiled at Chelsea, her wide skirt blocking some kind of wheeled cart behind her. "Well, here we are. Aren't you pleased Ms. Kilcuddy has found you?"

Dr. Kendall stepped forward. "I think you have the wrong room."

Chelsea studied the woman without recognition. As the kindly-faced woman approached, Chelsea's apprehension increased accordingly. And she had no idea why.

The look in Ms. Kilcuddy's expressive eyes changed from delight to puzzlement. "Isn't this Chelsea Connors's room?"

Excitement sent adrenaline surging through Chelsea. This must be someone she knew. This woman could help her, perhaps lead her to family or friends.

"I'm Chelsea."

With difficulty, the woman turned around, bent and picked up a bundle and turned back to offer it to Chelsea. "My dear, this is your little boy."

# Chapter Two

A perfectly manicured forefinger and thumb picked an imperceptible speck of dust off a mahogany desktop. If the damned dog hadn't pulled out the stake and come to Chelsea's rescue, she wouldn't still be breathing.

But mistakes could be rectified.

Finding Chelsea again hadn't been easy. But a resourceful planner had ways of ferreting out information. At the first phone call, she'd been listed as Jane Doe. Persistence, another round of phone calls and a few lies to a nurse had won the day.

Chelsea Connors had all the luck, landing in cushy Maryland Memorial. The hospital had regulations, security and locked doors, but that wouldn't keep out a determined person.

Her diagnosis of amnesia had turned out to be a stroke of luck. That meant she couldn't identify anyone, including her attacker.

But since she might regain her memory at any time, following through with the plan with all due haste had become a necessity. Chelsea Connors couldn't hide or run from her fate.

She'd only prolonged the inevitable.

"MY BABY?" Chelsea stared at the infant, baffled by the squirming bundle. What kind of mother didn't recognize her child?

The baby's head looked perfectly round and disproportionately large for the short body and stubby legs. A cap of curly light brown hair framed large blue eyes, a button nose and plump pink cheeks.

Chelsea sat up in bed. "He's mine?"

The hefty woman placed the baby in Chelsea's arms. "Of course, dear."

Naturally she didn't remember a thing. But her memory wasn't a priority right now, not with the cuddly infant in her arms. A scent of powder wafted up to her nostrils, and she hesitantly reached down to smooth the infant's darling curls. So soft. So sweet. So helpless.

While she fumbled with the bundle and awkwardly caressed the child's cheeks, Dr. Kendall frowned. "Ma'am, how did you get a baby into this hospital?"

Ms. Kilcuddy winked and smiled broadly. "Where there's a will, there's a way." She handed Chelsea a file of papers. "This little tyke has been separated from his mother long enough."

"I don't understand," Chelsea said, setting the file beside her unread.

The woman's smile wavered, and she pointed to the file. "You went before the judge and signed the custody papers last week, dear. Surely you haven't forgotten?"

"Chelsea was hit on the head," Dr. Kendall explained. "Her memory has not yet returned."

Ms. Kilcuddy's smile faltered, and her eyes grew large with sympathy. "Oh, you poor thing. If there's anything I can do, you just let me know. I'm sure you and Alex will do just fine together.''

Panic rose to choke Chelsea. Holding the wiggling baby didn't feel natural. Alex couldn't be hers. Surely she wouldn't be so inept if she'd done this before. ''You're sure this is my child?''

Ms. Kilcuddy sighed, and her large bosom heaved. ''Oh yes, dear. The courts check out parents quite thoroughly before ordering foster care to turn over a child to a new parent.''

Chelsea's brow wrinkled in confusion. Why was her baby in foster care?

A nurse tried to enter the room, and Dr. Kendall walked to the door, said something in her ear. The nurse left with a smile, as if pleased to do the handsome Dr. Kendall a favor. When he pressed his back to the door, blocking anyone else from interrupting, Chelsea wanted to drape her arms around his neck and kiss him for giving her the opportunity to get to the bottom of this new puzzle. Instead, she settled for a glance of appreciation.

Questions swam fast and furiously through her head. How had this woman ended up with her child? And what had she meant about gaining custody? Had Chelsea recently divorced? ''How did you find me here? Why did you have my baby?''

The woman looked from Dr. Kendall to Chelsea. ''Oh, you poor thing. I'll explain what I know, but it's not a lot.''

''It would be a great kindness.'' Dr. Kendall's voice was cordial, but Chelsea noted the flicker of impatience in his eyes that indicated he was as eager to hear the answers as she was.

Ms. Kilcuddy leaned forward and tickled the baby under the chin. "I don't want to upset you, but Alex's mother was Anne Spears, your best friend. She was murdered."

Murdered. Her best friend was dead. And she couldn't remember her face, couldn't recall the pain she must have felt at her loss. Chelsea gulped in a lungful of air.

She wasn't the baby's birth mother. No wonder the little darling didn't feel right in her arms. No wonder she felt so unfamiliar with the idea of motherhood.

Ignoring Chelsea's startled reaction, Ms. Kilcuddy continued. "Anne Spears had been mugged and died without recovering consciousness from a coma. It's a shame her attacker has yet to be apprehended. But life goes on. In her will, Anne requested that you adopt her baby. You agreed. Last week you signed for custody. When you didn't show for your appointment to pick up Alex, I suspected something was wrong. I called every hospital in the area and tracked you here."

"What about the baby's father?" Dr. Kendall asked.

The woman from foster care shook her head sadly. "Poor little tyke. Only three months old. Anne named Albert Marcel Llewellyn as the birth father on Alex's birth certificate."

Albert Marcel Llewellyn. The name didn't mean a thing to Chelsea.

"The court made every effort to find Mr. Llewellyn but failed. That's why we had Alex in our care for so long. Actually Alex was accidently given to Barrett Montgomery, and the little tyke even made it to Walt Disney World. But that's all straightened out now.

Baby Rachel is back with Zoey and Barrett, and you have your little guy safe and sound."

Rachel? Zoey? Barrett? The names meant nothing to Chelsea. She squeezed the baby. Besides being orphaned, at three months he'd already been a victim of government ineptitude. "Alex doesn't have a mother or a father?"

At the sound of Chelsea's voice, Alex screwed up his face and screamed, his mouth puckering in a tight little twist. Jiggling the baby only made the yowls increase until her ears rang.

"He may not have his natural parents, but now he has you, dear."

Yeah. He had her. The poor kid didn't have any luck. Not only had he lost his parents, he'd ended up with a mother who'd lost her memory and had no idea how to care for a child. She would never have guessed such loud noises could come from someone so small. Alex's eyes squeezed shut tightly, and his face flushed crimson. Enormous tears rained down his cheeks.

Dr. Kendall approached, and Ms. Kilcuddy placed a business card beside the bed. "I've told you all I know, but if I can help, you can reach me at this number." When Ms. Kilcuddy leaned forward to kiss Alex goodbye, she whispered in Chelsea's ear, "The handsome doctor is showing more than a gleam of interest in you, dear." Then with a wink and a swish of her skirts, she was gone, and Chelsea hoped she wasn't blushing at the woman's words.

Alex cried as if he knew he'd been left alone again.

With her lack of knowledge, Chelsea looked to Dr. Kendall for help. "What do I do?"

He lifted the baby from Chelsea and tucked Alex near his side, supporting the baby's head in the crook of his elbow. "What's wrong, tiger? Are you alone and scared? No need to be. The pretty lady's going to take good care of you."

Chelsea tucked away his compliment and the warm feeling it evoked into a memory file to draw out and examine at another time. She couldn't help smiling as Dr. Kendall spoke to the baby.

"You're going to have a wonderful life, little fellow."

Alex ceased his caterwauling and stared at the doctor as if fascinated by his face. Surely a three-month-old baby couldn't distinguish between handsome and ugly? But how could Chelsea ignore the evidence before her eyes? With barely a few soft words, the doctor had enchanted the baby with his charms.

Maybe he knew a doctor trick. "How did you do that?"

As he made goo-goo eyes at Alex, Dr. Kendall sculpted his lips into a silly grin. "How did I do what?"

"Get him to stop crying."

"I just made him comfortable by supporting his back and head. You'll get the hang of it in no time."

Despite his words, he showed no inclination to hand the baby back. Instead, he clicked his tongue against the roof of his mouth, and, fascinated, the baby cooed in appreciation. When Dr. Kendall ran a finger along the sole of his tiny foot, Alex smiled a toothless grin, showing off a deep dimple in each cheek.

Chelsea chuckled. "I think he likes you."

"I'm a likable kind of guy, aren't I, tiger?" He jiggled his dark brows, and the baby waved a tiny fist.

Chelsea didn't know the good doctor well, but people of all sizes and ages—even babies—seemed to agree. There was nothing not to like about Dr. Kendall.

The baby reached for the stethoscope, missed and slapped the doctor's face. Dr. Kendall chuckled softly. "Ah, tiger, you want to be a lover not a fighter."

Chelsea giggled. "You sound odd, talking to him when he can't understand a word you say."

"He understands more than you might think—not my words but my tone. In a few days he'll recognize you and smile when you walk into his room. He'll tell you without words when he's hungry or needs a diaper changed."

Chelsea settled against a pillow and arched a brow in skepticism. "How?"

"You see, babies . . ."

She might find the topic fascinating but she still couldn't hold back a yawn. Dr. Kendall returned to her side with Alex comfortably nestled on his shoulder. "You can learn all about babies later when you aren't exhausted. What you need to understand now is that Alex can't remain here."

"Why not?"

"Hospital policy forbids healthy children from staying with their parents. I'll have to call child services."

"Child services?"

"No need for alarm. It's a government agency. Whenever a family member is unavailable to watch the children, family services helps out. They'll send someone to care for him until you are able."

"But—"

"Relax. After we call, they take hours to come to the hospital. Since it's almost five o'clock, I doubt they'll show until tomorrow." He winked. "And you can check out tomorrow."

She should trust her instincts instead of jumping to conclusions. "Thank you, Doctor."

"Meanwhile, I'll see to Alex's care." He smiled at the infant. "Come on, tiger. Your new mama needs rest."

Jeff carried the baby toward the nursery in hope of prevailing on one of the nurses to take care of Alex. The baby snuggled against him, content to suck his thumb.

"That's it, Alex. You just relax. If I can find Nurse Betty or Nurse Allison, I'll be leaving you in the best of hands."

The baby didn't seem anywhere near as tired as Chelsea had been. He turned his head as people walked by, his eyes alert and curious.

With the baby quiet in his arms, Jeff focused his thoughts on his patient—his too-attractive patient. Alone and scared, she'd gazed at him, fighting back tears, and he'd had difficulty maintaining his professional distance. It wasn't just her pretty face that made him want to reach out and comfort her. If he analyzed her features one by one, he wouldn't call her a true beauty—her lips were a tad too full, but perfect for kissing. Her large eyes eclipsed a short, straight nose and perfect white teeth in an oval face. Her skin, smooth and clear, was too pale for his taste, but after what she'd been through, she'd held up remarkably well—surprisingly well. Feature by feature, she was not extraordinary, but with looks and character combined, she was a fascinating mix of strength, vulnerability and mystery.

After watching her cope admirably with a loss of identity that would floor most patients, he suspected during normal times Chelsea Connors was a collected and cool customer. She might appear vulnerable on the surface, but beneath he sensed a core of steel.

Because of the head wound, he couldn't have sedated her if she'd become hysterical. His only option would have been to restrain her. Thank God, with her strong will dominating her fear, it hadn't come to that.

Jeff longed to know Chelsea Connors better. But as long as she remained his patient, he had no choice in the matter. Theirs could only be a professional doctor-patient relationship. Chelsea had been injured, she'd been in a coma for a day and now she had amnesia. She needed time to recover.

Yet it was peculiar that so minor an injury had caused Chelsea's amnesia. Psychological trauma was more likely responsible.

Although it hadn't been his place to voice his suspicions to the cop, Chelsea was clearly in trouble. While the mystery surrounding her intrigued Jeff, the gun she'd purchased was an indication she was involved in something dangerous and possibly deadly.

He walked down the hall, noting the nurse who had been flirting with Officer Russo was now hanging on his arm. Strangely, or maybe not so strangely, the blond policeman was still around. When he spotted Jeff and the baby, he separated himself from the nurse and made a beeline for Jeff.

Officer Russo whipped out pen and paper in a gesture more suited to an ace reporter than a lawman. "Spare a minute, Doc? Ms. Kilcuddy filled me in, but I have a few more questions."

Jeff took the man's elbow and steered him to a visitors' waiting area out of the traffic of the busy corridor. "Sure."

Tiny sucking noises emitted from Alex's throat. His bright gaze settled on Russo's chrome pen.

"About your patient, do you believe she has amnesia?"

"Why would she fake it?" Jeff countered.

"There's all kinds of reasons. She could have had a fight with a boyfriend and needed a place to hide out. She could have killed someone with her missing gun. She could be crazy."

"She's not crazy. Her actions are those of a determined, logical and frightened woman."

"Exactly my point, Doc. But what's she got to be scared of?"

"Imagine waking up in a hospital. Your head hurts. You can't remember how you got there, what happened to you or who you are. Have you any idea how frightening it must be to have no family, no friends, no roots?"

"But could she be fooling you?" Russo pressed. "You don't have physical proof of her amnesia, do you?"

Jeff had had enough aspersions cast on his patient. Drawing himself up to his full six feet plus, he wrapped himself in a forbidding air of professionalism. "Do you think she faked a coma, too?"

"You tell me. Is that possible?"

Alex squirmed and Jeff shifted the baby to his other arm. "EEG's don't lie."

"What about her head wound?"

"What about it?" Chelsea had enough problems without being badgered by the cop. Alex indicated a restlessness by waving his arms, so Jeff rested him against his shoulder.

"What caused the injury?"

"It's impossible to say. She could have fallen or been struck from behind."

"What about the bruises on her arm?"

"She probably sustained those when she fell." Alex burped and Jeff rubbed his back. "Is there something you aren't telling me?"

Russo shrugged with irritating nonchalance. "Seems like a big coincidence that she had the accident at the same house where her best friend was murdered."

Jeff hid his reaction to that statement behind his professional calm. He didn't like the man's insinuation. He seemed to be implying Chelsea was somehow responsible for her own injury. All his protective instincts rose, and his eyes narrowed. "Then maybe you should be checking out the neighbors as carefully as my patient. Is that all, Officer? This little fellow needs to be put to bed."

Alex yawned and burped again.

The officer hitched his pants over his stomach. "I'll be in touch."

As Russo strode away, the baby spit up. Just as Jeff had thought, the baby was wound up tight from all the moving around he'd been doing.

"Yeah, little guy, this whole situation is making me sick to my stomach, too."

He hurried toward the nursery, unable to banish doubts about Chelsea. True to his profession, the police officer had assumed a worst-case scenario, but his patient's wounds were typical of someone who'd pitched forward and struck her head, using her arms at the last minute to break her fall.

But just because she hadn't been attacked didn't mean she hadn't been in trouble. And she had more unanswered questions about her life and background than a resident could ask a first-year student during rounds.

To make matters worse, Jeff had a bad feeling about the missing gun.

DESPITE CHELSEA'S exhaustion, she didn't immediately fall asleep after Dr. Kendall left with Alex. As she struggled to make sense of what had happened since she'd awakened in the hospital, her thoughts swirled like snowflakes that refused to settle on a windy day.

The amnesia left her without a foundation from which to view the world. She could hear, smell, see, taste and touch, but each sensation seemed new and fresh, with no basis for comparison in her past—like a new or altered reality.

What was a person without the sum of her life's experiences? Without memories to anchor her, she was lost, alone, afraid.

*Stop it.*

She had her health, her intellect, her instincts. Until her memories returned, she would survive with what she had. She'd rest, regain her strength and think of ways to search out clues about herself.

Once she returned home, she would seek out her past. Surely she would find people who could tell her what she needed to know. She would have to be patient. She grinned, somehow suspecting she'd never mastered that particular virtue.

Perhaps she could use her amnesia to develop new qualities. Like a blind person depending on their hearing, she would have to develop other instincts and respond to small clues to make up for her memory loss. Instead of a handicap, she should consider her lack of memory a chance to view her life with fresh vision.

Her past was like a slate wiped clean—no, not quite. There were some mysteries that carried over from her past to her present. Like why she'd been carrying a gun.

Picturing a weapon compact enough to fit in her purse, she tried to fill in the missing details. Had she learned how to use the weapon? Was the gun black or chrome? What had happened to it? Not one mental picture returned.

Relief that the gun was no longer in her possession seeped through her. Hoping the missing weapon never turned up, she shuddered, unable to master her instinctive revulsion. Besides, a weapon would be dangerous with a child living with her.

Chelsea pictured the baby's face, his bright, inquisitive eyes, his darling dimples and lashes already long enough to flirt. And her baby was smart. When she had held him, Alex had obviously recognized Chelsea's inexperience. Her lack of confidence had made Alex insecure.

Ah, but she would learn. Her mothering instinct was strong. She'd heard some mothers bonded the first time they held their child. She could well believe it. Although the little bundle had seemed awkward in her arms, she already hungered to hold him again.

Alex wasn't yet too mobile, and that should make caring for him easier. He couldn't sit up or crawl. And she shouldn't need a master's in education to keep a baby fed, diapered and bathed. Of course, sharing the responsibility would be easier if the baby had a father.

Alex deserved a man like Dr. Jeffrey Kendall—gentle, understanding yet protective. The doctor had gone out of his way to help without being condescending. He'd held Alex with the ease of experience. Those goofy faces he'd made had ended the baby's tears and endeared him to Chelsea. Who would not admire a man who didn't mind appearing silly to stop a baby's cries?

Was Dr. Kendall accustomed to children because he was a physician? Or did he have kids at home?

She didn't recall seeing a wedding ring. But she wouldn't make assumptions. Perhaps a band of gold wouldn't fit beneath the latex gloves doctors wore during operations.

The almost inaudible beeping of the heart monitor relaxed her. With visions of Dr. Kendall pushing the baby on a swing, Chelsea drifted into exhausted sleep.

She dreamed a perfect film commercial, the kind where years flash by in snapshots. Alex's first tooth, his kindergarten graduation, standing on a podium in a swimsuit with a winner's ribbon around his neck, prom night with a date, a wedding.

Suddenly, amid dancing wedding guests, a demon arose, its eyes shooting red flames. The guests panicked, running, screaming and diving out windows. Chelsea tried to run, but her feet were rooted to the floor.

Just when she thought the flames would singe her, the demon turned into a woman's face. She had sad eyes, crinkled at the corners, brown hair twisted back in a ponytail, and she kept licking her thin lips.

"You promised me," she whispered, her voice and image beginning to fade.

"What?" Chelsea asked, confused.

The voice weakened further. "You promised me. Don't break your word."

"What? What did I promise?" Chelsea shouted. But although the woman tried to answer, Chelsea couldn't hear her words.

She must have cried aloud, disturbing her sleep. She wakened in a sweat, breathing hard. In her dark room, she took several seconds to realize she'd been having a nightmare.

The faint smell of antiseptic, mixed with the fresh scent of clean sheets, slapped her back to reality. The soft light of the monitor lit the room in a green glow.

She was safe.

Her name was Chelsea Connors, and she was in Maryland Memorial Hospital. Snuggling under the covers, she tried to go back to sleep.

Nothing could hurt her in bed.

She was safe.

Already the nightmare faded, and she let the images go without regret. The pounding in her head had eased a bit. She shifted slightly to find a more comfortable position and opened her eyes to see a hazy lab coat.

Was a nurse in her room to give her a shot? No. The professional white coat wouldn't fool her. The person hovering over her was too still, too silent and creepy.

Someone was in her room, someone who was not supposed to be there. Her mouth went dry. A dark silhouette loomed over her bed, and her gut twisted into barbed-wire knots.

As she stared, trying to pierce the darkness, an arm was raised in a threatening gesture. The hand clasped a hypodermic needle, its sharp metallic point glinting in the green light. The arm sliced downward, the hypodermic needle aimed at her chest.

# Chapter Three

If Chelsea didn't move fast, she'd die. Seizing the IV tubing, she wrapped it around her hand. As the hypodermic arced toward her, she yanked the IV pole, slamming it against the dark silhouette in the lab coat. A soft thud was followed by a groan.

Chelsea rolled off the bed, and the sticky pads ripped off her chest. The IV had long since torn from her hand. She hit the floor on hands and knees, striking her head against the side of the bed with a thwack. Sharp, stinging pain bit into her scalp. Head whirling and lungs desperate for air, she scrambled away, any moment expecting her assailant to grab her to complete the attack.

Too dizzy to attempt to stand, she scrambled to the corner of the room. The heart monitor emitted one long, flat beep. Surely someone would come to investigate.

Her thin gown didn't protect her from the chilled tile where she huddled on the floor. She bit her lip to keep her teeth from chattering, but she couldn't control her shivering.

*Somebody help. The baby needs me.*

She tried to scream, but fear paralyzed her throat. Her head spun, and she clenched her fingers deep into her shins to stay conscious.

Piercing lights came on. She squinted against the brightness, momentarily blinded.

*Please, no. Don't let that hypodermic needle stab me.*

Hands reached for her. Her vocal cords eked out a frightened whimper.

"Take it easy." She recognized Dr. Kendall's voice.

Shaking and still unable to speak in a normal tone, she croaked out in a voice no louder than a whisper, "Did you see who it was?"

At her frantic words, she read bewilderment on the face of the nurse, as well as on Dr. Kendall's. With sinking disappointment mixed with fear, she realized they hadn't seen anyone exit her room.

"Someone sneaked into my room. If I hadn't rolled off the bed, I'd be dead."

From the long look the nurse and doctor exchanged over her head, she figured they didn't believe her. But it had happened. She would never forget the sight of that evil weapon slicing down at her. Closing her mouth, she forced down the hysteria rising in her throat.

"You're going to be fine." Dr. Kendall put his arm around her waist and helped her to stand. "Breathe. Take three deep breaths."

She did as he asked, but every nerve in her body twitched with tension. Her knees buckled. Dr. Kendall picked her up and strode toward the bed, his concentration clearly on her bleeding hand, not her story.

"Get a pressure bandage, stat," he ordered a nurse. "And call security."

At least he was giving her the benefit of the doubt. That she'd get a chance to explain her story took the edge off her panic.

Dr. Kendall's solid strength comforted her. "Are you okay?"

"Please, I'd like to sit in a chair for a moment." Her head still spun, but she had to gather her thoughts so she wouldn't sound crazy when she spoke.

After he helped her into the chair, he reached for her hand. "Let me see your hand." Concern darkened his eyes.

The icy tile chilled her feet, contrasting with the heat where his fingers grazed her just below the elbow. Longing to crawl into his arms and let him reassure her again with his warmth, she fought the inclination to depend on him. Dr. Kendall wouldn't always be there. She had to learn to be strong, at least for Alex's sake if not her own.

The nurse returned, and the doctor tended the tiny injury on her hand, then asked her to use her free hand to apply pressure to her wound to stop the bleeding. While she responded, Chelsea forced herself to recall the terrifying assault. Afraid of discovery, her attacker must have left her room and fled the moment she'd fallen. Could the hypodermic, with fingerprints, have been left behind?

Still trembling, she slouched in her chair and released the pressure on her wound. Her scalp was damp with perspiration, and she raked shaky fingers through her bangs.

Dr. Kendall reached for the bandage on her head. "I need to look at this, too."

At his touch, she winced. "I slammed my head when I rolled off the bed."

He replaced the bandage, so she couldn't be in too bad a shape. Hoping he'd believe her but knowing she might sound like a nut case, she wondered if she should tell the truth and risk being locked in the psycho ward. But then whoever had tried to kill her might return.

"Security should be here any minute. Luckily you didn't open the stitches in your head."

"Stitches?" He hadn't mentioned them before. No wonder she felt as if she'd been scalped. "How many stitches?"

"Only three. We hardly had to shave your hair."

Her hair was the least of her worries. Someone had tried to kill her! She stiffened, wondering if her slip on the steps had been a mere accident. Could her "slip" be related to the attack in the hospital?

Sinking her face into her palms, she counted to ten to calm herself. The delay didn't help. If she'd been attacked once, perhaps twice, it could happen again.

*Stop.* She couldn't let her imagination run rampant. She'd been jumping to conclusions without facts or memories to back them up. The incident had frightened her enough without her imagination scaring her silly and making matters worse. Still, she couldn't stay in the hospital.

"I should get out of here."

Dr. Kendall patted her shoulder. "We won't let anything happen to you."

At the sound of footsteps, Chelsea lifted her head. A man, bald and slightly overweight, wearing a blue uniform with a walkie-talkie at his belt, sauntered into the room. "Is there a problem, miss?"

"Someone tried to attack me." Chelsea spoke as calmly as she could, but her tone lacked the strength of conviction she would have liked.

The security guard pulled the radio from his belt. "What did the assailant look like?"

She twisted her hands in her lap to still the shaking. "I don't know. The lights were out, and it was dark."

"Was it a man or woman? White or black? Tall or short?"

"All I saw was a white lab coat and a murky shadow."

From the discreet look the guard shared with the doctor, she knew she'd said the wrong thing. At best, they didn't believe her. At worst, they thought she was a mental case.

"Tell us what you can," Dr. Kendall suggested gently.

"I was sleeping. Something woke me."

The guard frowned. "What? A noise? A voice? The door opening?"

She shrugged, then wished she hadn't as her head throbbed. "I was having a nightmare."

The guard shook his head and rolled his eyes at the ceiling.

Dr. Kendall didn't give up as easily. "Go on."

"When I opened my eyes, there was this hulking presence looming over me."

"You're sure you were awake?" asked the guard.

"Positive. The green light from the monitor glinted on a hypodermic needle." Quickly she filled him in, trying to keep calm and sound rational when she wanted to run and shout.

Although he clearly didn't believe her, the security guard searched the bed sheets and the floor under her mattress, looking for the needle. "Nothing, miss. Doc, you want me to file a report?"

"No one on staff saw anyone leave this room. Without a description, I don't see what good it can do. Thanks for coming."

The men were humoring her. After the door closed, she let some of her agitation show in her tone. "You don't believe me. You think I imagined it, don't you?"

"Head trauma can cause vivid nightmares. Nightmares that *seem* real."

"I was awake," she insisted. Hell, she could have died. And if he wouldn't believe her, she'd just have to make it out of here on her own. Standing, she held on to the back of her chair for support and tested her balance.

He stepped to her side. "Let me help."

"I'm not getting back into that bed." She shuddered. "I couldn't sleep a wink, knowing he could return."

"He?"

"He or she. I'm not sure." She turned to him, suspecting how difficult it would be to leave but knowing it was imperative. "I want to check out of the hospital immediately. Whoever attacked me could return."

The vehemence of her tone warned Jeff that Chelsea could be stubborn. Still he tried to talk her out of leaving. "We can protect you here. Alex is in the nursery, all tucked in. You sure you want us to release you, alone, in the middle of the night?" he asked, reluctant to let her go.

If she wanted to leave, hospital policy would force Jeff to go along with her wishes. Yet her walking out into the night, without a friend, with a baby to care for, seemed more than she should have to manage. Her face was pale, her respiration labored, and she was trembling from her fingers to her toes.

And yet she'd stood up to him with more courage than any patient he could remember. Trying to convince himself he wanted to keep her in Maryland Memorial because of her amnesia and not because he found her courage appealing, he tested her resolve.

"Are you prepared to take care of a baby?"

"I don't know. And I may not know tomorrow or the next day, either. I can't stay here forever."

He gazed into eyes greener than ivy and read her determination. Her chin tilted at a bold angle, and her full lips pressed into a decisive line.

"You could use some rest."

"I'll rest after I'm at home, behind a locked door." She preferred to flee now just in case anyone who meant her harm thought to retrace his or her steps. Most likely her attacker would assume she would spend the remainder of the night in the hospital.

He searched her eyes and noted the dark shadows beneath them, took in her vulnerability, looked deeper and found a steely core below. Obviously nothing he could say would sway her. Still he could not quite give her up.

"I was hoping by tomorrow someone might come to claim you."

"Someone already has recognized me." She ticked people off on her fingers. "The woman from foster care—oh, and let's not forget the person who tried to stab my heart with a hypodermic."

She seemed sure she hadn't dreamed the incident, and the thought bothered him. Although her memory was absent, her perceptions were acute. By her sarcasm, she'd revealed her awareness that he'd humored her after she'd claimed to have been attacked.

She must have picked up the frown he'd tried to conceal. "Doctor, with all the people coming and going down the halls, with staff—from nurses to janitors—having access to my room, I assure you I'll be safer elsewhere, behind a locked door. Now, where are my clothes?"

There was nothing to be done but help her. While he went in search of Alex, she changed. He returned to find her dressed in a green silk blouse, spotted with dried blood from her head wound, and a rumpled cream skirt.

As he wheeled her out of the hospital and to a taxi, a nurse pushed the baby in his stroller alongside them, and he fought to keep his gaze off Chelsea's legs. Fought and lost. She had the legs of a dancer, firm, long and sculpted.

Her special mix of defenselessness and courage heightened his every protective instinct. Letting her leave was against his better judgment. Longing to jump in the cab and accompany her home, he resisted.

*She's trouble. Let her go.* In an hour he'd be so occupied with his next patient he'd forget all about Chelsea Connors and her amnesia.

His beeper signaled he was needed in ICU.

And still the cab arrived too soon. Jeff slipped a twenty-dollar bill into her hand, collapsed the stroller into a car seat and strapped the baby beside her. Although he'd made up his mind to forget her, the thought of never seeing her again bothered him more than he wanted to admit. "You're sure about this?"

"Thank you."

He wanted to press a kiss to her cheek. "Don't forget, those stitches need to come out in about a week. If you have any problems, headaches, disturbing nightmares, anything, don't hesitate to call."

"I won't."

His gaze dropped to Alex. "Take care of that little tiger."

"I will," she mouthed as the cab pulled away. She waved, her thoughts tight with sadness. Alex started to cry. Right now Dr. Kendall seemed their only friend in the world, and the baby must have picked up on her feelings of loss, her anxiety about their destination, her fear that she hadn't the knowledge to care for a baby.

"Where to, ma'am?" the driver asked.

She flipped open her wallet and tilted it toward a passing streetlight. "Twenty-six Carson Street."

At least the driver didn't make her feel worse by asking her to give directions she couldn't recall. She had enough worries wondering who had attacked her at the hospital and why. If she was lucky, the assault had been random, committed by a deranged stranger. And if she wasn't lucky, then she had to be very careful.

The baby needed her, depended on her to make the correct decisions. The motion of the car rocked Alex, who plopped a finger into his mouth and sucked. She had to remember to buy a pacifier.

Smoothing Alex's hair, Chelsea leaned back in the seat and closed her eyes, certain she'd never been so tired in her life. Yet she couldn't sleep with her mind full of worries. What kind of home would she find when she arrived? An apartment, a condo, a house? She hoped for secure locks on the doors. Despite her fear of guns, she needed to be able to defend herself and Alex, and she wished for the missing gun to show up.

She could find herself married and the mother of children. Was she a good enough actress to fool her kids into thinking she recognized them?

The thought of facing a husband who was a stranger made the hair on the back of her neck rise. If confronted, somehow she would dredge up the strength to answer questions, like where she'd been for the past day and a half, but it wouldn't be easy.

The best-case scenario would find her living with a childhood friend who could fill her in on the past twenty-odd years of her life. Or parents who would help with Alex. Perhaps a boyfriend who made his living as a bodyguard might be too much to ask. But until she set her life back in order, she couldn't let the baby suffer because of her ignorance.

Behind them a vehicle honked. Chelsea jerked straight with a start. Turning, she looked behind them, her eyes widening with fear. A full-size van rudely flicked on its high beams and caught them in a glare of bright light.

The van rode the cab's tail, almost close enough to ram them. Had she been followed from the hospital? She reached for Alex.

*Please, no.* Not now with the baby beside her.

As if in answer to her silent plea, the van jerked to the side, passed the car, then cut in front of them. The cab driver muttered an oath.

As the van sped into the night and left them behind, Chelsea released her pent-up breath. A rude stranger—nothing more—had almost run them off the road. It happened every day. No one had singled her out to follow.

Wondering if the knock on her head had made her paranoid or prudent, she sat back with frustration at her gripping fear. Why couldn't she remember? If someone was stalking her, she wanted to know why. Perhaps no one was after her at all, and the attack at the hospital had been a nightmare, her fall a simple accident.

Yeah, right.

Dr. Kendall had seemed so sure she'd dreamed the attack. But he was wrong. The image of the hypodermic needle slashing toward her chest was just as vivid as her memory of Dr. Kendall's vibrant blue eyes, his concerned demeanor and the glimmer of masculine interest he couldn't conceal.

Had she imagined his personal attention? No. Although she suspected he treated all his patients with consideration, a special spark had arced between them.

Perhaps after she settled and her memory returned, she'd be free to give the good doctor a call. The thought had come to her easily, and she wondered if she often asked men out on dates. Whatever her experience, she knew a man like Dr. Kendall didn't remain so long at every patient's bedside.

Before she had time to dwell further on Dr. Kendall, the cab driver turned off the highway into an upscale neighborhood. One-and two-story Colonial houses with lush oaks and landscaped yards were set back on acre lots. Tension eased from Chelsea's shoulders. This subdivision would be the perfect place to raise a son. The cab's headlights spotted swing sets in several yards, and a bike path ran beside wide sidewalks.

She paid and tipped the driver, who helped transform the car seat back into a stroller. Keys in hand, she rolled the sleeping Alex toward the front door of an unfamiliar brick house. There were no lights on inside. If anyone was there, they'd long since gone to sleep.

She hesitated on the doorstep. Overhead, dark, billowing clouds obscured the moon. The air, dank and humid, closed in to smother her. Crickets chirped in the late-summer heat, and sweat trickled under her arms. If not for Alex, she might have run. What and whom would she find inside her house?

What would she do if she found someone in her bed?

Shoving the possibility from her mind, she inserted a key in the lock, trying two before she used the right one. She eased the carriage over the threshold into a dark foyer lined with boxes labeled with black lettering that told her the contents held Alex's belongings. The faint scent of pine and a crisp silence greeted her. Chelsea fumbled for the light switch, hoping it wouldn't wake the baby.

That thought became moot when a siren screamed. Damn! Damn! Damn! She'd set off an alarm.

Alex woke and began to cry. Before the alarm alerted the entire neighborhood to her homecoming, Chelsea hurried to the hall closet, flung open the door and reached for the numbered kill switch. And groaned.

She couldn't remember the code to silence the wailing siren. She barely restrained her tears. Why could she recall where the alarm box was but not how to turn it off?

Of course, she couldn't recollect the name of the security company, either. Resigned but frustrated, she plucked the crying baby from his stroller, awkwardly placed Alex against her shoulder and stepped outside to wait for the police.

Lights flashed on in the house across the street. But no one came to ask about her safety, which led her to believe she wasn't overly friendly with her neighbors.

An hour later, the police had checked the empty house, silenced the alarm and gone. Alex was still screaming.

The house seemed to be in an L-shaped configuration and featured a sheltered courtyard and windowed, south-facing wall. Warm buff dominated the interior walls in a monochromatic blend of textures and styles.

She brought the baby into the airy den amid a collection of antiques and headed toward a French chest that matched the subdued shade of green on the dining-room and living-room ceilings. Stepping across glowing floors of heart pine, she took pleasure in a pair of lamps made from Regency candlesticks and topped with shades of Cowtan fabric. Apparently well-loved elements, a champagne cooler, a French bronze lamp and a Chinese porcelain plate rested together on a Portuguese console. A glance out back showed a shimmering pool next to what looked like a wisteria-covered arbor.

Chelsea wrinkled her nose. A pungent odor emanated from Alex. The smell grew stronger. A dirty diaper. Is that why he wouldn't stop crying?

Remembering how he'd responded to Dr. Kendall's voice, she tried to talk to him. "I'll clean you up. Give me a moment." She carried him back into the hallway full of boxes. "All we have to do is find a diaper."

Her voice made no good impression on the baby. He cried even louder.

In the boxes by the door, she found washcloths, baby shampoo, powder and soap. There were linens for a crib, bibs, and clothing—but no diapers.

Carrying Alex with one hand and a box of supplies with the other, she dumped the carton on the kitchen counter by the sink. Next she spread out a clean towel, placed the baby atop it and ran the lukewarm water into the sink.

Feeling efficient and organized yet inept, she removed the diaper. While she held her breath, she pinched the soiled plastic between two fingers and dumped it into the trash. She used a wipe on his cute little bottom, dusted him with powder and then patted his soft tummy. Alex kicked in protest the entire time.

"What? What's wrong, little guy?"

She racked her brain, wondering what mothers used before disposable diapers were invented. What else could go wrong? He should have stopped crying. Could he have colic? Appendicitis?

Keeping her voice even was difficult with his wails grating on her eardrums. "Come on, Alex. Give it a rest."

She picked him up, ignoring the powder on her blouse and carried him down the back hall toward what must be the bedroom. Opening the first closet door she came to, she found hand towels. If she possessed a sewing kit and safety pins for a makeshift diaper, she hadn't a clue where to look for them.

Returning to the kitchen, she laid Alex back on the counter. Perhaps she could tie the towel ends about his hips and fashion a diaper.

"You don't have to fight me." His arms thrashed like a freestyler's in an Olympic race. Holding his hips steady was next to impossible. "Come on, baby. Hold still."

Alex's legs churned like an egg beater. In his rage, his face turned from pink to deep crimson.

When a rap on the front door sounded, Chelsea jumped. Her mouth turned dry. Suppose the attacker from the hospital had followed her here?

When she picked up the infant, the cloth slipped past his knees. One kick, and the towel fell to the floor. And she considered sitting down right there next to the towel and crying along with Alex.

At another knock, she straightened her back, shoved aside her sudden apprehension about someone at her door at this time of night and carried the half-naked baby to the hall.

Suddenly, warm liquid seeped down the front of her blouse. "Oh, Alex. You didn't..."

She peered down at her blouse and groaned. "You did."

Odd noises, a thump, a groan, a bang, seeped through the door.

"Who is it?" she called.

When no one answered, a chill worried its way down her spine and deep into her stomach. She couldn't hide and pretend no one was home—not with Alex screaming like a banshee.

She shouted the first thing that came to mind. "Don't try anything funny. The house is surrounded by police."

"I would have noticed that, ma'am," a deep voice answered from the other side of the door. "After all, I'm out here and you're in there."

From the hallway, she flipped on the exterior porch light. At two more sharp thumps at the bottom of the door, she glanced through the peephole. At first sight of someone sinister, she would call 911.

"Dr. Kendall!"

She recalled her earlier words about police surrounding the property, and blood heated her cheeks. She hurried to unlock the door and wondered why he was here. No one was sick, unless she counted the ache in her palpitating heart.

"I thought—" She started to apologize, then stopped in surprise. Her reaction to him was so swift and violent. He had come to her home, at night, and except for the baby they were alone. Her former panic turned into another kind of tension. Her insides jangled at the sight of him, making her feel like a breathless teen.

"It's okay." His gaze traveled over her face and searched her eyes. "Are you all right?"

"Marvelous," she muttered, her sarcasm covering her giddy sense of pleasure at seeing him again.

As relief and excitement helped the knots in her stomach unwind, she opened the front door wider. "Come in. You scared the daylights out of me. I wasn't expecting . . ."

Dr. Kendall must have kicked the door with his foot. Both hands were full. He looked terrific in crisp navy jeans that hugged lean hips, his shoulders more than filling out a white button-down shirt open at the collar. Tearing her gaze from the tempting V and the fine hairs curling below his neck, she took in the packages he was juggling. His clean-cut look impressed her. But what won her over was the gallon of rocky-road ice cream and a jar of fudge in the bag wedged beneath one arm. He carried in both hands a large basket laden with formula, a pacifier and a rattle.

She reached out and took the almost-falling bag balanced between the basket and his chest, peeked inside and found a jar of maraschino cherries. But when the huge box in the middle of the basket caught her attention, her lips split into a wide grin. "You brought diapers!"

If she hadn't been so tired and her head wasn't pounding, she would have danced an Irish jig. "Dr. Kendall, thank you. Thank you. Thank you."

"Call me Jeff. And you're welcome." He laughed, his rich baritone low and throaty. Alex's head turned, but he didn't stop crying.

Her blouse dripped onto her skirt. Spinning on her heel, she didn't wait for Jeff but fled to the kitchen, calling over her shoulder, "We had a little accident."

She wrapped a towel around the baby, and as Jeff entered the kitchen she gave up mopping her ruined blouse with a paper towel. Wishing she could have looked great instead of standing in a sopping blouse, stinking of baby pee, she shot him a frazzled grin of welcome.

"And you brought ice cream. Yum." Right now she'd love a little sugar to boost her energy.

Jeff's eyes danced with amusement. "Why don't you go clean up, and I'll take over for a while."

Now, that was an offer she couldn't refuse. Not that there was much about Dr. Jeffrey Kendall she wanted to resist. His charming blend of male-model good looks and thoughtfulness was a knockout combination. *Careful.* She had to remember her past before she could have Jeff in her future. And in the present, the baby needed attention. "First, please check Alex. He's been screaming for a while. Is he okay?"

Jeff glanced at the crying baby. "He'll be fine. It's you I'm worried about."

Gingerly she handed him the wailing infant. "I really don't know how to thank you."

His eyes warmed and his mouth turned up in a smile that sent a reviving sizzle straight to her toes. "I'll think of something." The heated look in his eyes radiated intimacy and left her with a fuzzy warmth rushing through her veins.

He shooed her on. "Go. And remember not to get those stitches wet."

The master suite encompassed a sleek, clean-lined glamour that appealed to her. And a single dresser. Relief that she needn't confront a husband flooded her.

Reminiscent of Park Avenue heiresses in the twenties, devil-may-care images created by early film-makers decorated the walls. Sharply defined silk window treatments, plush wool-velour carpeting and a pattern of warm grays and taupes added to the room's glamorous tones. Although none of it seemed familiar, the room soothed her.

She showered quickly, unwilling to take advantage of Jeff's generosity. She had no right to be thinking the things she did about the handsome doctor. She sighed. He'd probably stopped by just to see if she was okay. No doubt he believed it his duty to follow up on his patient and was anxious to be on his way. He probably thought he'd released a lunatic to take care of Alex and worried over the baby's safety. Although this scenario wasn't flattering, she couldn't blame him for wondering about her mental health.

Even without a full memory, she knew that doctors didn't make midnight house calls. Dr. Kendall—Jeff, she amended—was a rare individual in the way he cared for his patients. They hadn't yet had a chance to talk, and she hoped he'd come to tell her they'd caught her attacker.

She opened the closet to confront an array of strange clothes. Riffling through the hangers, she felt like a shopper in a department store, except she already knew every garment would fit. Thankful there were no men's clothes next to hers, she brushed her fingers along the soft fabrics until she found some casual items.

As she changed into jeans and a kelly knit sweatshirt that would bring out the green in her eyes, she tried to ignore the reason she was primping. After dabbing on lip gloss, she hurried back to Jeff to see how he was managing with Alex.

She shouldn't have worried. Jeff had everything under control. He sat in the recliner, a diapered Alex in his arms. The baby, eyes closed, was sucking down the last drops of formula.

His bold gaze flickered over her. "You look great."

"Thanks." She spoke in a normal tone that belied the sudden squirmy sensations his compliment had caused.

"I came to apologize."

"What for?" She met his direct gaze with a curious one of her own.

"After I got off duty, I started thinking and realized I should have taken your story of an intruder more seriously."

She forced herself to squelch the hope that he was here for another reason than an apology. "Hey, it's okay. I probably wouldn't have believed me, either."

The phone rang, its shrill tone cutting the peaceful scene like a scalpel. A call at midnight couldn't possibly be good news. An icy prickle trickled down her back.

She took a deep breath and picked up the phone. "Hello."

"You owe me. I'm coming to collect." The whispered threat sounded more ominous than a shout.

# Chapter Four

She slammed the phone down in the cradle. The blood drained from her face. Again she wished for her missing gun. Perhaps she'd even bought the weapon because she'd been receiving threatening phone calls.

Jeff, tough and lean, came to her side without waking Alex. "What happened?"

"Just a crank call."

The phone rang again and she jumped, her pulse racing.

With a commanding air of self-confidence, Jeff reached for the phone an instant before she did. "Hello."

She held her breath.

He dropped the receiver back into its cradle. "They hung up."

"Did they say anything?"

"No." His brow creased with worry. "Did someone threaten you?"

She repeated the words, sure she'd never forget them or the sick feeling in the hollow of her stomach at the threat. "The person said, 'You owe me. I'm coming to collect.'"

"Was the voice a man or a woman?"

"I don't know. They whispered in a raspy tone."

"Maybe we should call the police," Jeff suggested.

Chelsea's voice quivered. "What is happening to me? What was I involved in before the accident?"

"Don't worry," Jeff soothed. "I'm not going anywhere until we get some answers."

Jeff hadn't asked if he could spend the night; he'd told her. And while his take-charge attitude should have made Chelsea's need for independence rise up and refuse his help, she had Alex's safety to think about. If anything happened to her, who'd look after the baby?

Besides, she was scared. Someone had tried to attack her, and now she'd been threatened. So although she wasn't sure if she liked Jeff taking control, with her memory loss, the incident in the hospital and now this menacing phone call, she'd be foolish to deny his offer of additional protection. Especially when she had no idea why she'd bought a gun.

If she could find out more about herself, she might discover who was threatening her, what she owed the caller and why she didn't have enough change in her wallet to pay a toll. If it hadn't been for Jeff's generosity, she wouldn't have had cab fare.

He'd already helped her so much, she wasn't sure how she'd have managed without him. So despite his forceful statement, she gave him a jittery smile. "Are you sure staying is not too much trouble?"

"No problem."

"It was likely just a crank call." She didn't believe her own words but she wanted to sound rational and calm instead of on the verge of panic.

"Probably. But I couldn't sleep if I drove away and left you alone." He glanced down at the sleeping baby. "Where do you want the little guy?"

"I saw a crib in the back bedroom."

"I'll see to him." Jeff jerked his thumb at the kitchen desk. "You might want to check the answering machine. You've got some messages."

She walked over to the machine and pressed the Playback button with anticipation, hoping to finally hear some clues to her predicament. "The library books on order have come in. Please pick them up within three working days."

She tapped her foot while waiting for a beep, then a woman spoke in a businesslike tone. "This is Sandy. Don't forget your appointment tomorrow."

Jeff returned, opened the freezer and removed the ice cream. "Who's Sandy?"

"I don't know." Her frustration seethed until she thought she'd boil over. She hadn't learned much. Only now she had more questions that needed answers. "And I hope my appointment isn't important."

If he heard the disappointment in her tone, he ignored it. Making himself at home in her kitchen, he stuck the jar of fudge in the microwave and took two bowls out of a cabinet. "How much hot fudge did you say you wanted on your sundae?"

"Lots." It might take a gallon to cheer her, but she appreciated the effort he was making.

His grin was irresistibly devastating. "And four cherries on top?"

"You have a good memory. So tell me, Doctor—" she gestured to the bowl of ice cream he'd offered, and she kept her tone light as if his answer would mean little to her ''—do all your patients get this kind of treatment?''

Light smoldered in his blue-flecked eyes as he moved toward her. ''Ah, Chelsea. You are no longer my patient.'' His husky whisper offered as much promise as warning, and she felt as if her breath had been cut off.

She swallowed hard and bit her lip until it throbbed like her pulse. The taste of hot fudge was almost forgotten. With just a few words, he'd kindled a hunger for something much sweeter.

He dipped his head, and his lips touched hers. A mere brush of flesh. But there was nothing ''mere'' about the desire flaring within her. And it was too much for her to handle. Too soon to be kissing this man when she couldn't remember if she was promised to another.

Awkwardly she moved away, fleeing what she wanted most, trying to channel the restless energy slicing through her into another activity. ''I need to keep looking for clues.''

Banking the desire in his eyes, accepting the limits she'd set, he let her change the subject as if he recognized how uncomfortable she was with her own feelings. While they spoke, she searched the desk in her kitchen for her missing gun, a personal phone directory, a clue to why she'd been attacked and threatened. Names and phone numbers would be a great place to start looking for answers about her past. Instead, she found menus for take-out food delivery.

Giving up on the desk with a sigh, she wandered into the connecting den and talked to Jeff through the pass-through above the bar. ''There are no photographs on the walls.''

"Keep looking."

She opened a door in the den that led to the two-car garage and stuck her head inside. "Empty. The police officer said my car is still over at Anne's house." After one glance at the papers Ms. Kilcuddy had given her, she'd recognized Anne's address as the same one where her accident had taken place and an inexplicable fear tightened her chest.

"I'll give you a ride over there to pick it up tomorrow."

For a moment, she felt as though she had an angel watching out for her to compensate for everything else she was going through. "Thanks." What was she thinking? No angel had such boldly handsome features and such confident sensuality.

Avoiding his gaze and uncomfortable with the direction her thoughts kept taking, she opened the doors to a lavish wall entertainment center. "No photo albums, just stacks of magazines."

"What kind?"

"Decorating, landscaping, architecture. High fashion, entertainment and a television guide."

"Sounds like you're well-read." He joined her, handing her the unfinished sundae. "Maybe you kept a journal or diary in the bedroom."

"I'm going to tear this place apart from top to bottom. There have to be answers somewhere." She glanced at the mantel over the fireplace. "What kind of woman doesn't have pictures of family?"

"Maybe someone who doesn't have a camera."

She scooped up a mouthful of rocky road and let the chocolate melt over her tongue. "Or someone with something to hide."

He sat on one end of the mahogany-trimmed humpback sofa and raised his bowl in a salute. "This flavor ice cream is good stuff. As for the photos, maybe your family's house burned down and you had to start over."

She took the library chair opposite him. The entire conversation didn't seem real to her, as if they spoke about someone else, unconnected to her in every way. Except she couldn't let her memory loss and sense of isolation deter her from figuring out the truth. Her life might depend on what she discovered. "Possibly I don't have a family."

"Maybe you're the kind of person who carries memories in her heart."

His words caused a lump to rise in her throat. Unwilling to let him know how much his tender words touched her, she hid behind silence.

With a mischievous grin, he rescued one of his cherries from an avalanche of hot fudge and held it by the stem above her lips. "Maybe this will sweeten your thoughts."

She leaned forward, took the cherry between her lips and plucked the fruit from the stem between his fingers. "Mmm." If only she could accomplish everything she wanted by simply making a request. "I didn't find any additional clues to my identity in the bedroom, either." She swallowed the cherry with a small sigh. "This house reminds me of a model home."

"Because of the decorating?"

"Because there's no mail, no magazines, no pictures." And she still hadn't found her missing gun. "This house could belong to anyone. It's a showpiece without warmth."

"I don't know." His eyes twinkled. "It seems middling warm to me. Of course, you could raise the temperature if you sat here." He patted the spot on the sofa beside him.

Something in his blue eyes dared her to take a chance. After that brief kiss, cuddling against him held an appeal too strong to deny. But even as she scooted beside him, her thigh pressed to his, she wondered if encouraging him was a mistake. His charm could distract her when she should be concentrating on finding out who had threatened her. "You realize I could be married."

"I don't think so. You don't wear a ring." He spooned up the last of his hot fudge, a thoughtful glint in his eyes. "Did you find any male clothing in the bedroom? A pair of extralarge slippers beside the bed? A set of dentures by the bathroom sink?"

"I might have been such a horrible wife, my husband moved out and left me."

It felt good to lean on him, and she put her problems aside for a moment. He curled his arm over her shoulder, and she snuggled against him, breathing in his spicy scent of bay rum cologne.

He licked the last of the hot fudge off his spoon. "Then again, you might have murdered your ex-husband and thrown away the gun."

She jerked in his arms and lightly punched his shoulder. "That's not funny."

He didn't let up his teasing. "Or maybe since the bill collectors call here in the middle of the night, you're after my money."

Her body molded itself to his contours. Weary and yet oddly alive and optimistic, she sighed contentedly and let him cradle her against his side. "I didn't think interns earned much."

"We don't. My grandmother left me a trust fund."

She chuckled, enjoying the way he'd made light of her amnesia until her worries seemed ridiculous. And she appreciated that as appealing as the thought was, he wasn't pressing her for another kiss. Right now she needed comfort—not raging hormones she was unprepared to handle. "So I faked my amnesia to meet a young and rich doctor?" She reached up to her bandage. "I assure you, if I was that hard up for a date, placing an ad in the personal section would have been easier. I can just see my ad now. 'Wanted, rich intern who specializes in mystery women and has experience with baby boys.'"

"Is that why you let me stay? My experience with children?"

"Sure." She swallowed the last bite of her ice cream, pushed away her thoughts of a stalker just outside her front door and teased him in return. "Do you want to play Mrs. Doubtfire?"

He wiggled his brows. "I'd rather play doctor."

She laughed, her pulse racing, but she returned the topic to safer ground. "Where did you learn so much about kids?"

She yawned, and it seemed natural to place her head on his shoulder. His hand soothingly caressed her upper arm. "I have six brothers and sisters."

"Let me guess. You're the oldest."

"Yeah. Dad's a cardiac surgeon. He wasn't around much, so I used to help Mom with the little ones."

"And you intend to follow in your father's footsteps?" She yawned again.

He kissed her forehead. "Enough conversation, sleepyhead. I think you're ready for bed. Don't worry about me, I'll take the couch."

"But—" She rose to her feet.

He rested his palm in the small of her back and gave her a gentle push in the direction of her room. "Go. You need sleep. Doctor's orders."

Exhausted, she did as he suggested, instinctively knowing Jeff wouldn't come on to her unless she was ready. She looked in on Alex, who slept sucking his thumb. She admired a handmade pillow in bright colors that matched the draperies, thinking the room had been only half-prepared for a baby, since the shelves meant for toys were still empty. Too tired to dwell on what she couldn't remember, she staggered to bed. The minute her head hit the pillow and she closed her eyes, she fell asleep.

She awakened the next morning to the phone ringing on the nightstand. Opening her eyes, she sneaked a look at her clock. Seven a.m. Sleepily she reached for the receiver.

"Hello."

"You aren't *still* in bed?" The woman sounded horrified. "You're late for the staff meeting. If you don't leave soon, you'll miss your eight-o'clock."

She bolted upright. Eight-o'clock what? The puzzle swept away the last of her sleepiness. Chelsea matched and identified the voice on the phone with the one on her answering machine. "Sandy?"

"Yes."

"I had an accident yesterday." Chelsea paused and thought hard. How much should she tell this woman?

"Are you okay?" Sandy sounded efficient, not overly concerned.

Oh, yeah, she was okay, all right. She'd lost her memory, discovered she was a mother, been attacked and received a threatening phone call. Life was just peachy.

Chelsea kept her sarcasm to herself. "I've a few stitches in my scalp, nothing that won't heal in a week." She thought it odd the other woman didn't ask what happened, and continued, "But I've forgotten some things. The good news is the doctors expect my memory to return to normal in a day or two."

Alex started to fuss, but Chelsea heard Jeff's footsteps and then his husky voice murmuring to the baby. She shouldn't leave the care of the child to him, and yet this phone call was her first link to someone who could tell her something about her life. Sandy might even know why the phone caller last night had said Chelsea owed him or her.

She gripped the receiver tighter. "Sandy, are we friends?"

"When you hired me, you said we were to have only a business relationship. You wanted a secretary to do what she was told and to keep her nose out of your personal affairs."

Chelsea winced. "That sounds...cold."

"Our relationship is professional. Have I done something wrong?"

"Uh, no. Nothing like that." Unwilling to admit too much yet, Chelsea dug for more information. "Tell me about my eight-o'clock appointment."

"It's with Mark Lindstrom at Benedict Academy."

Her secretary wasn't exactly forthcoming with information. But then Chelsea was supposed to know the details. She opened a drawer to her nightstand and pulled out a pad and pen. Beneath the pad rested a personal phone directory. Finally! She'd found a clue that might lead her to discover what kind of trouble she was in. Her pulse raced at the possibilities.

She forced her mind back to the conversation. "Can the meeting be delayed?"

"Do you want to risk losing him? Surely you haven't forgotten the near-fiasco the last time we put him off?"

Of course she had forgotten. But forewarned, she wouldn't repeat the mistake. Chelsea excitedly flipped pages while they spoke, realizing the book contained a wealth of information—if only she could decipher her notation system. "Memory of my recent business deals are a little shaky. What's at stake?"

Sandy sounded puzzled, as if she thought Chelsea was testing her. "The solvency of this firm depends upon your sewing up the account. Your appointment is crucial."

Great. Winding her finger around the phone cord, Chelsea contained a groan. She didn't know what business she worked for or what her job was, but the firm could go bankrupt if she didn't land the account. So what else could go wrong?

She took a deep breath and let out the air slowly. "Please explain to Mr. Lindstrom that I spent yesterday afternoon in the hospital and ask him to reschedule for ten o'clock. I'll just have to miss the staff meeting. Could someone fill me in?"

Her remarks were met with a long, taut silence. She must have said something out of character.

Finally Sandy spoke. "Without you, there is no staff meeting. Have you forgotten you *own* Classy Creations?"

*Damn.* She'd made a vital mistake. Now, despite her reluctance, she'd have to say more than she would have liked. "Uh, Sandy. I'm going to level with you. I'd appreciate if you keep what I'm about to say confidential."

"That's why you hired me. I can keep a secret."

"Good. I have total amnesia."

Sandy gasped. "What happened?"

"I'll explain when I get to work. If there's a problem with rescheduling Mr. Lindstrom, please get back to me. Otherwise, I'll see you at ten."

"Yes, Ms. Connors."

Chelsea didn't want to alarm her employee or make obvious changes until her memory returned. Yet at the same time she desperately needed her secretary to apprise her of the other employees, the business, her plans. In short, she needed a friend. "Sandy, how long have we known one another?"

"Three years."

"Then call me Chelsea, okay?"

"Yes, ma'am."

Chelsea hung up the phone, wrote the name of her firm, Classy Creations, on a memo pad conveniently placed by her bed. She'd look up the company's address in the phone book, call a cab and see what she could discover about her life. For the first time since she'd lost her memory, she was eager to go forward.

With a good night's sleep, the day seemed brighter, like an adventure about to begin. And last night's horror she pushed to the back of her mind. The throbbing in her head had almost disappeared. She threw a bathrobe over her T-shirt and, with the personal planner in hand, she followed the smell of perking coffee to the kitchen.

A pitcher of orange juice sat on the table. Waffles popped out of the toaster. Some hostess she was—she hadn't even cooked breakfast or helped make up Jeff's bed last night. She'd left him to find his own linens, and he was the one who'd gotten up to tend the baby.

Jeff sat in the rocker feeding little Alex the last of a bottle. Alex wore a cute jumpsuit with a red-and-white-striped shirt. Not only had Jeff fed the baby, but he'd probably changed his diaper, too.

And he'd taken over her responsibilities without losing one whit of his masculine appeal. Jeff's clothes weren't the least bit rumpled, and she wondered if he'd slept in his shorts or nude.

An image of his golden skin amid rumpled sheets heated her cheeks. *Don't think it,* she sternly ordered herself. She couldn't get involved—not until her memories returned and she knew her own mind. Not until she found out who was behind the attack at the hospital and the nasty phone call last night.

With a charming smile, he glanced at her as she entered the kitchen. "Good morning. Did you sleep well?"

"Yes." After a few false starts, she found the right cabinets and took out plates, silverware and cups to set the table. "What about you? The sofa couldn't have been comfortable."

"I can sleep anywhere. It's a trick I learned to get through med school. But you have a guest bedroom. I slept next to Alex. The little guy didn't let out a peep all night."

"How am I going to thank you for everything?" She waved her hand in a gesture that encompassed Alex.

"I've been thinking about that." In the soft morning light, Jeff's blue eyes twinkled, looking more mischievous than she remembered. Recalling the solid feel of him against her on the couch, somehow she knew she'd enjoy whatever he'd conjure.

Picking up Alex, Jeffrey placed him over his shoulder and rubbed the baby's back. "Today is my last day of work before vacation. I intend to celebrate the end of this rotation over dinner at the Crab Café. Come with me?"

"After all you've done, I should be cooking you dinner." She frowned. "But then I'm not sure if I know how to cook."

He laughed, his rich chuckle bathing her in a warm glow. His skin was sun kissed, as if he'd spent the summer sailing on Chesapeake Bay and not in the hospital. But what she liked most about his features were the tiny laugh lines radiating from the corners of his brilliant blue eyes, crinkles that indicated he laughed easily and often.

"I'll pick you up at seven. You should be fine surrounded by co-workers." His eyes blazed with banked embers. "But I'll still be thinking about you."

His concern, mixed with decidedly male interest, shot a warm rush of heat through her. "Is the restaurant nearby?"

"Actually it's closer to town."

"No need for you to drive out of your way. Why don't I meet you there?"

Alex burped and drew their attention.

"If you don't have a sitter, bring the little guy, too."

She nodded agreement, her palms itching to carry the baby again. She yearned to cling to Alex fiercely, not because the baby needed reassuring, but because she ached to hold someone. "Here, I'll take Alex so you can eat."

She went to Jeff, and he handed her the baby. She still held Alex a bit awkwardly but soon rearranged her arm in a natural position. His little body snuggled against her waist. Mimicking the way Jeff carried Alex, she almost felt comfortable.

She half expected Alex to scream. But the baby seemed fascinated with her robe. His tiny fingers rubbed against the velour as if he couldn't get enough of the silky feel.

Did the baby miss his mother? How horrible for Anne not to live long enough to see her child grow to adulthood. And the poor little fellow would never have memories of his birth mother.

Chelsea vowed to find out all she could about Anne so she could tell Alex stories when he was old enough to understand. Hopefully the police would bring Anne's murderer to justice long before Alex began asking awkward questions.

Jeff spread a baby blanket over the floor and drew her from her thoughts. He placed a rattle and a stuffed teddy bear on the blanket. "You need to eat, too. Put him on his tummy by the toys. He's too young to wiggle much."

She did as he said, oddly reluctant to release the soft bundle. "How long until he can crawl?"

"Each baby is different. He'll be up on his hands and knees rocking first. You'll have plenty of warning before he's mobile. Some babies are good wiggle worms, though Alex seems content to stay in one place for now. Enjoy it. Once he's on the move, he'll be a handful."

Over breakfast she ate and flipped through the pages of her appointment book. Apparently she used initials to identify people. W.B. and M.L. were used frequently, along with several others, and she guessed these to be business related.

One notation did stick out. Two months ago, she'd written "Obsession," circled it and underlined it three times. But she had no idea to what the word referred. It seemed both ironic and irritating that every time she learned something about herself, she had not fewer but more questions that needed answers.

Trying to put the puzzle behind her, she told Jeff about Sandy's call. And her missed eight-o'clock.

"What are you going to do with Alex?" he asked.

"Take him with me. Apparently I own the company, so I won't be fired for lack of child care."

Jeff raised a cup of black coffee to his lips. "And what do you do for a living?"

"I'm not sure. The name of the firm is Classy Creations."

"You could design anything from furniture to houses to clothes."

And "Obsession" could refer to the name of a perfume or a line of clothing, a book or even a movie.

She paused, a piece of waffle drizzled with syrup halfway to her mouth, wishing she could decipher her shorthand notes on the calendar inside the personal planner. "My secretary said this meeting is important. After I find my office, am I going to know how to do my job?"

"Absolutely." Jeff's confidence quelled her budding panic. "You may not remember your client or employee names, but work is part of your experience. You'll be able to draw on your store of knowledge."

"That's good news."

He sighed, pushed away his empty plate and placed his elbows on the table, leaning forward. "But I should warn you, if you're in the decorating business, you may not remember the color of the material you ordered last week."

The sinking sensation in her stomach was back again. "I don't understand."

"If you were a doctor, you'd know how to perform the operation, but you wouldn't necessarily remember the patient or the patient's illness."

She opened the personal directory to the phone numbers. "I suppose that's why these names mean nothing to me. I didn't find any relatives listed under Connors."

"That doesn't necessarily mean you don't have family. The numbers you call often probably aren't written down."

Chelsea cleared the table and put the plates in the dishwasher. "I know. But the list is mostly businesses. I'm beginning to wonder if I have friends. I suppose I'll find out once I get to work."

"Scared?"

"A little." For a stranger, Jeff read her well, but even he couldn't guess the trepidation she faced going to work today. She could come face-to-face with whoever had attempted to stab her with that syringe and she wouldn't know it.

As much as she wanted to stay home and hide, she would discover more around people who knew her. Deciding that amnesia made her vulnerable, she decided to limit the number of employees who knew about her problem to an essential few.

While she wiped off the counter, Jeff flipped the pages to the calendar and appointment scheduler in the back. "On the date you were brought to the hospital, it says, 'Pick up Alex.' On Thursday, 'Day cleared for Alex.' And look, your meeting for today is right here." He pointed.

Chelsea glanced down. "M.L. Important." The words were written larger and bolder than the other notes. "Well, I guess I'll find out what that means when I get to Classy Creations."

She'd intended to call a taxi to take her to work. Sometime today she had to track down her car. After dinner she hoped to take Jeff up on his offer to drive her to Anne's house. But after she dressed, Alex drooled on her, and Jeff ended up driving her to Classy Creations.

He parked outside a striking gray-stoned building. He handed her the day planner, and their fingers grazed. At his touch, a brief shiver rippled through her, and her heart beat with the pulse of the pop radio station's music. "Would you like me to come inside with you?"

*Yes.* "No, thanks." His closeness was so male, so bracing, but she had to stand on her own despite her fear of the unknown. She waved goodbye to Jeff, glad that she planned to meet him later.

The name Classy Creations was written in white neon over the etched-glass doors, giving no hint to what kind of business she owned. Urging herself forward with the hope that the familiar surroundings might jog her memory, she advanced, her mouth dry. Pushing Alex in his stroller, she entered the elegant three-story office building.

Chelsea intended to find Sandy and regretted her failure to ask her secretary where her office was located within the building. Stopping by the elevator, she read a placard and learned Chelsea Connors, president, had taken the entire third floor for an office. Before moving on, she noted her vice president's name was Martin Tinsdale, accounting was run by Walter Brund, her art director was Micki Lawson and her traffic manager, Sandy Ronald. The names meant nothing, but she suspected several names matched the initials in her personal planner. She didn't even try to remember the myriad of account executives or assistant account executives. Waiting for the elevator, Chelsea straightened her skirt and matching navy jacket with its double row of brass buttons and wondered if she looked like she usually did. Earlier, she'd removed the bandage and combed her hair over the stitches so no one should even suspect she'd been hurt. Ignoring her nervousness, she hoped Alex's presence would distract her employees from noticing their boss's uneasiness.

Except for the small mishap before they left the house, the baby was behaving himself. He seemed fascinated with the welcoming potted plants and the modern lighting reflecting off the darkly inviting mirrors in the lush entrance. Unfortunately she recognized none of the decor.

The elevator opened and two people stepped out, one of them greeting her with familiarity, the other more formally. She stiffened as they approached and had to force herself to stand her ground and pretend normalcy.

"Hello, Ms. Connors," said a pert redheaded girl who couldn't yet be out of her teens. Although her tone was bright and cheerful, the girl refused to meet her gaze. Was she shy at talking to the boss? Or was Chelsea simply so on edge that she bordered on paranoia?

A skinny man with four gold earrings in his left ear smiled and spoke in a distinctly feminine tone. "Beautiful baby, Chelsea."

"Good morning." She hoped her general greeting would be enough and the man and girl would pass by without stopping to talk.

"I'll have the layout ready in a few minutes, Mick," the young girl said as she sauntered away.

Mick. He must be her art director, and she wondered if he always walked with a slight limp.

He stopped beside her, seemingly intent on a private conversation, and she suddenly felt too alone and exposed in the otherwise vacant hallway.

"The mock-ups are set, and the color work looks spectacular." He kissed his fingers. "That new graphic free-lancer is top-notch."

She had to quit overreacting. When Mick didn't immediately leap and attack her, she concentrated on his words and settled for a safe reply. "Good."

Mick gave her a thumbs-up. "Good luck. You know where to find me if you need me."

Did Mick's preparations have something to do with her appointment? Suddenly anxious to speak to Sandy and clear up the mystery, Chelsea pushed Alex into the elevator. They rose smoothly to the third floor. Mick had acted as if he knew about the baby, so she must have discussed Alex. She could assume others knew about him, too, so she wouldn't have to explain his presence.

Good. The less explaining she had to do, the better. Especially when she had so many questions.

She had fifteen minutes before her appointment. And she still didn't know what she did for a living. She felt like a downhill skier racing on thin ice. Only Jeff's certainty that she would know what she was doing gave her the confidence to proceed.

The elevator doors opened. Chelsea ignored the flapping butterfly wings in her stomach and pushed Alex and his stroller through the doorway. The scent of fresh roses welcomed her.

The third floor was silent, practically empty.

Free of hallways and partitions, the rooms flowed together without a ripple. The visual unity was reinforced by walls painted in a pale putty color and by a ceiling glazed in shades of green similar to the colors used at her house. Artfully placed French doors flooded the office with sunlight. A balcony overlooked a rear courtyard. Additional large clay pots, filled with healthy plants and vases of long-stemmed roses that matched those in the garden below, gave the spacious office a warm touch.

"There you are." A willowy brunette standing behind a lacquered desk shot her a wide-eyed look, shoved a few papers into her drawer and wiped an imaginary piece of dust off the spotless desktop with a fingertip sporting a one-inch, perfectly manicured nail.

Chelsea strode in her direction. "Sandy?"

"None other." Sandy lowered her contralto voice. "He's already here."

Chelsea didn't see anyone in the large room. "Who?"

"Your ten-o'clock appointment, Mark Lindstrom." Sandy glanced at the stroller and then tilted her head toward a wall that had been crafted so magnificently, the doorway was camouflaged. Chelsea could just barely discern what must be the inner sanctum, a smaller office off this large one.

"I'll watch the baby." Sandy reached for the stroller's handle.

Unsure why she was reluctant to leave Alex with her secretary, Chelsea decided to follow her instincts. "Thanks, but I'll keep him with me. He looks about ready for a nap."

"Fine." Sandy shoved a sheaf of papers into her hand. "I prepared a file on the campaign for you."

Her secretary was supposed to be answering questions, not creating new ones. Chelsea's brow furrowed. "Campaign? Is Lindstrom a politician?"

Sandy frowned and gave her an odd look. "He runs Benedict Academy."

Somehow Chelsea didn't think the prestigious military academy needed Classy Creations to redecorate. Opening the file, she read about her meeting with Mark Lindstrom last week at Benedict Academy.

Had she seen something at the military academy she shouldn't have? Her heart started thumping madly. Her thoughts sped in speculation. Perhaps the attack in the hospital and her missing gun were connected to her work. Could she be involved in a military secret or cover-up?

She took a deep, steadying breath. "Sandy?"

"Yes."

"What kind of business do I run?"

# Chapter Five

At Chelsea's question, Sandy clamped a hand to her mouth, cutting short her gasp of obvious dismay.

Chelsea touched the other woman's shoulder and tried to conceal from her voice her own frustration with her handicap. "I'm perfectly capable of work. I just need your help remembering what that work is."

"I don't understand," Sandy whispered.

"No one does. Now, please help me figure this out. What am I trying to sell Mr. Lindstrom?"

Sandy visibly recollected herself. "You call him Mark. And you're trying to sell him our advertising campaign. Classy Creations is a public-relations firm."

While Sandy spoke, Chelsea skimmed her writing and relief flooded through her. While she didn't recall the specifics, her thorough notes brought her up to speed on the 150-year-old military academy. Immediately upon reading, she understood the concept, the unique slant, the selling points in the presentation she was about to pitch.

"Thanks, Sandy. After I'm through, I want us to sit down and chat."

One perfectly plucked brown eyebrow arched. "Chat?"

"I think it would be best if you and I remain the only ones who are aware of my amnesia. I don't want the troops to lose confidence. So I'll need you to fill me in on the employees, the history of the firm, where we stand financially, our other clients—those sorts of things." And maybe her secretary knew about her personal life and why someone had tried to kill her.

"Yes, Ms. Connors."

"Please, call me Chelsea," she insisted again. "After three years, it's time we became better acquainted, don't you think?"

Sandy glanced pointedly at her watch. "I think you'd better not keep Mr. Lindstrom waiting. You know those military folks are prompt."

Chelsea had started to walk toward the back room when Sandy whispered, "The password on your computer is '$-M-O-N-E-Y-$.'"

What else? Besides business, there didn't seem to be much in her life. At least now she had Alex. "Thanks."

Wondering what other essential information she'd forgotten to ask, Chelsea gathered her courage. Could she pull this off? Perhaps she should admit her amnesia to her client, but then she'd certainly shake his confidence in the firm, and according to Sandy, Classy Creations couldn't afford to lose this account.

Once again Jeff's words came back to her. He'd said she would know her job. She damned well better. Her and Alex's future depended upon it.

She wheeled the stroller into the back office, thankful Alex was asleep. For once the little darling had excellent timing.

"Hi, Mark," she greeted the man standing so stiffly by the window that he could have been at attention except his hands were clasped behind his back. His shoulders filled an immaculately pressed uniform. His black shoes were polished to shine.

Mark Lindstrom was younger than she'd expected, maybe thirty. And he was handsome. His bold blue eyes behind wire-rimmed aviator glasses, square jaw and straight nose were pleasing to the eye. His dark hair with a light sprinkle of premature gray was trimmed to perfection. Yet he didn't make her feel warm inside the way Jeff did, and she was relieved to know she wasn't attracted to every handsome man she met.

"Good morning." His greeting, clipped and sparse, matched the man.

She glanced around the room, taking in the easel, the computer behind a desk and the kitchenette next to a minibar. "Sorry we had to reschedule. I hope the change didn't inconvenience you."

Mark removed his glasses, plucked a folded tissue from his pocket and cleaned the lenses in a small circular motion. "Your secretary said you'd been in the hospital. Are you all right?"

"I slipped and fell. Luckily I needed only three stitches."

Mark replaced the glasses on the bridge of his nose and glanced at the carriage. "Good-looking baby."

She acknowledged the compliment with a grin, proud as if she were his birth mother and responsible for his genes. "I just adopted Alex. Sorry, I haven't yet arranged for child care."

His fierce gaze left Alex to fix on her. "I work with cadets every day. I like children."

For some reason, his stare made her uncomfortable. Perhaps it was the way he peered down at her. "Please, have a seat. Would you like some coffee before we begin?"

"Nix on the coffee. And I prefer to stand." He smiled, but it didn't reach his eyes. "I think better on my feet."

Behind her back, she clenched and unclenched her fists. *Relax.*

Chelsea walked over to the storyboard covered with a cloth. Her notes in the file indicated what she would find there. *He'll never know I haven't seen the art.* Quickly she decided to present the concept, then allow the art to sell Classy Creations.

"With Benedict Academy's expansion, you need students—high-caliber students. The best way to recruit is to encourage women to enroll in your school."

When she paused for a reaction check, he didn't move. His face remained implacable, and not even his eyes flickered with encouragement.

Determined not to let him see her sweat, she continued in an even tone, "It's just a matter of time before someone forces the school to admit female students. Instead of the courts legislating Benedict Academy to accept young ladies, why not create an atmosphere that welcomes them?"

"Go on." Mark folded his arms across his chest. Not a good sign. His words might sound as though he was willing to hear her out, and her notes said they'd lightly touched on this angle before, but his body language told her he didn't like the idea.

*So sell him.* Her financial future was at stake. Alex's, too. She couldn't just give up. Not until she gave the presentation her best shot.

"We've created an advertising campaign directed at women. But before we go on, I want to mention the free publicity we can generate for your school if you accept this concept."

"Free?" His arms loosened, and he leaned onto the balls of his feet. His attitude had started to soften from his hard line of negativity.

*Good.* Chelsea had her client's complete attention. For the first time, she thought she might pull this off. "A campaign to recruit women would be unique."

She moved on to outline the advantages, explaining how talk-show hosts would be eager to promote this new opportunity. *Even better.* He now stared directly at her while she spoke. "I'd like to kick off the ad campaign with a party. We'll invite well-known alumni and the press. Women's magazines shall be our prime targets."

He removed his glasses and again cleaned them with the tissue. "This will increase our exposure?"

She decided the cleaning was a ritual he performed while he was thinking. Surely the office couldn't be that dusty.

"Mark, I'm hopeful we can put Benedict Academy on prime-time national news. And that kind of exposure will reduce the money you have to spend advertising."

When he uncrossed his arms, clasped them behind his back and strode toward the easel, she knew she had him hooked. The first-class artwork on the storyboard reeled him in. The deal was almost cinched. But a sale wasn't a sale until the client's money rested in her bank account.

Mark's chin jutted forward. "You realize the board of directors will have to approve this change in policy?"

She'd won him over. "I'll meet with the board if necessary. But to implement this plan by next fall, we have to move quickly for several reasons. One, we need to begin planning the party right away."

"Perhaps we could combine our anniversary party with the announcement."

"Good idea. And two, this year's high-school seniors will make their college selections for next year soon. Our data indicates the best students choose early."

Chelsea moved to the computer, typed in her password and called up the files. Suddenly she hit a glitch. She'd neglected to ask Sandy which file included the layouts for Benedict Academy's printed ads.

With Mark peering over her shoulder, she skimmed down the list quickly, attempting to keep the panic cornered in the back of her mind. She'd come too far to blow the presentation now. She tried a promising-looking file named "Benn.act" but it proved to be the statistics used to compile her presentation.

Deciding a straightforward explanation would be the least suspicious, she pushed her chair back from the desk. "I've forgotten which file holds your advertising. Excuse me for a minute."

Hoping Mark wouldn't notice she had an intercom on the desk, she hurried on shaking legs from the office in search of Sandy, whom she found watering plants and cleaning dead leaves out of clay pots, and quickly told her what she needed.

Her secretary emptied the pitcher of water onto some ferns. "Try the 'Print.Ben' file."

Her stomach settled a bit. "Thanks. It's going well."

Sandy's startled eyes opened wide, and Chelsea realized she didn't usually give her secretary a running commentary of her progress.

Suddenly Sandy grinned and gave her a thumbs-up signal. "The contract is in the back of the file folder I gave you."

Chelsea confidently returned to her office to find Mark staring at a sleeping Alex. "Perhaps in eighteen years, he'll enroll at Benedict Academy."

"I'd want my son to attend a coed college. Admitting women may increase your applications from men."

Mark seemed to like that idea, too, and she made a note of it. Following Sandy's advice, Chelsea found the complete file. On the oversize monitor, the printed ads leapt off the screen, drawing the eye to the spectacular colors. Mick, her art director, had been right. The color mock-ups were fantastic.

"I'm impressed." Mark nodded as she paged down through a series of ads expressing the theme of welcoming women to the famed military school.

She gave him time to absorb and appreciate the simple elegance of the clean copy. Finally, she handed him the contract. "Your board of directors will want to review these numbers."

"They usually follow my recommendations." He took the contract without glancing at it. "We'd considered the issue of admitting women to our program before you suggested this slant."

"It's progress, the wave of the future. You can't go wrong to capitalize on it."

Opening his briefcase, he slid the contract into a pocket folder, careful not to wrinkle a page or so much as bend a corner. Briskly he shut the case and spun the lock.

"Thank you, Chelsea. I should be back to you within the week."

When they shook hands, his palm was cold, just like the man. "I'll look forward to hearing from you."

As he gripped her hand firmly, he looked into her eyes. And she felt nothing but satisfaction of a pitch well delivered. Mark's blue eyes didn't give her that same warm, fuzzy sensation in the pit of her stomach that Jeff's did. Yet both men were handsome. What made one man so appealing while the other left her indifferent?

Jeff's and Mark's looks might one day disappear. Yet Jeff would still retain his wonderful mixture of humor and compassion because those traits were inherent to his character. As she accompanied Mark toward the door of the inner sanctum, she realized how much she preferred Jeff's casual grace to Mark's stiff marching. If she had to depend on a man in a crunch, she'd much prefer Jeff at her side.

When they walked by the stroller, Alex cooed. Chelsea hesitated, wanting to see Mark out but reluctant to leave the baby.

"I can see myself out." Mark glanced down at Alex, who was busily stuffing the corner of his blanket into his mouth. "Looks like someone's hungry."

Chelsea chuckled. "I'd better feed the little fellow."

She picked up the baby, noticed he needed a diaper change and pulled a bottle of formula out of the bag beneath the stroller. As she popped off the nipple and set the bottle in the microwave next to the minibar, she spied Mark talking with her secretary. She supposed a little interest in Sandy couldn't hurt to win the Benedict account.

*Listen to me.* Her thoughts sounded cold, as if she approved of any behavior to win an account. Is that how she'd built this firm at such a relatively young age? Perhaps her heartless attitude had created an enemy that now wanted her dead.

As she changed Alex's diaper, she recalled the reactions of the few employees she'd met. *Respectful* characterized the way they treated her. While *dislike* might be too strong a word, *indifference* might be accurate. But indifference didn't drive someone to murder. What she needed was information about herself and her past, and she intended to find out more at the first opportunity.

Taking the bottle out of the microwave, she replaced the nipple and tested the warmth of the formula on her wrist. Alex spied the bottle and waved his arms with enthusiasm.

"I'm going to feed you, tiger. Let's take you over by the desk so I can read while you feed."

But the reports on her desk didn't hold her attention. Repeatedly her gaze wandered to the tiny bundle in her arms. Since just before he'd come into her life, she'd had trouble: her amnesia, then an attempt on her life and the phone calls that hinted that the danger was still there. But little Alex was the innocent party in all this. With his fingers curled into his palms, his tiny fists clutched the bottle. Blue eyes stared straight into hers while he sucked down his second breakfast.

And while she dug into her past, she couldn't neglect him. She intended to work through lunch, but perhaps this afternoon she could take time out to purchase additional diapers and formula. Jeff had bought enough to last a few days, but she'd already learned that running out could prove disastrous.

"There's a phone call from your attorney on line one." Sandy's voice startled the baby, and the nipple popped out of his mouth. Gently she eased it back in before picking up the phone and punching the correct button.

*Now what?* "Hello."

"I've got good news and bad news. Which do you want first?"

She gripped the receiver tighter. "Just tell me."

"The bank agreed not to start foreclosure proceedings. So we've bought you some time."

This was the good news? She held back a gasp. "How long?"

"Thirty days. Can you sew up the Benedict account by then?"

"I think so." Should she confide in her attorney and mention her amnesia? Her palms grew sweaty, and her fingers slipped on the bottle.

"I talked my partner into waiting to send our invoice."

They'd never agree to wait for their money if they thought someone wanted her dead. *Don't tell him.* Let them think everything is under control. Sure, everything was just fine and dandy if she didn't think about someone trying to kill her. "And the bad news?"

"Mary and Tom Carpenter's attorney called me again."

Again? Little clues she picked up reminded her that just because a subject was news to her didn't mean she hadn't discussed the situation with others. But who were Mary and Tom Carpenter?

"And?" she pressed, hoping to gather details without revealing her amnesia.

"The Carpenters are going to try and take Alex from you."

She almost dropped the phone. "What?"

"Since Mary is Anne's stepsister and part of a married couple, they want a chance to convince a judge they are better equipped than you to raise a child."

She gasped and blurted, "No!" Anne had left the baby to her, so the Carpenters probably hadn't been close to her. But Chelsea wondered if their claim to Alex might be valid.

Surprise entered her attorney's tone. "You don't want to settle?"

Had she indicated she'd be willing to give up the baby? She looked down at Alex in her lap. He'd finished his bottle and was trying to catch his toes with his fingers. Give him up without a fight? Never again feel his warm little body in her lap, smell the scent of his baby powder, watch his cheeks form those adorable dimples? Not a chance.

Her tone came out sharper than she intended. "No one is going to take Alex from me."

"Fine. Since your finances are strapped, I'll start delaying tactics."

"Can they win? Will their claim to Alex stand up against Anne's will?"

"I can't give you a guarantee. But we'll give them a full-fledged battle. Sure you won't change your mind?"

"Not this time." Chelsea cuddled Alex to her breast. She wanted to live long enough to help him grow to adulthood—not because she'd promised a friend she couldn't remember, but because the baby had brought a sweetness to life. He filled an emptiness she hadn't known existed. Because of Alex, she found herself looking forward to the coming years, and she'd found the courage to face her loss of memory instead of crawling into a hole to hide. "I won't change my mind. Some people grow on you."

JEFF SHOULDERED HIS WAY through the lunchtime crowd in the hospital cafeteria and set his tray down at a table for two. "How about some company?"

Garrick, the hospital's med-evac helicopter pilot, gestured with a callused palm to the extra chair. "Have a seat," he drawled with a Western twang. "Make any *grave* mistakes today?"

"Very funny."

The tall, broad-chested pilot laid aside his magazine and moved his tray to make room for Jeff. "We still on for tonight?"

Ever since Garrick had flown one of Jeff's emergency patients to the hospital rooftop last year, Jeff had considered him a friend. Although their backgrounds were similar, both being from wealthy families, Garrick came from a different part of the country. He'd grown up in the saddle on a ranch in New Mexico—a ranch so large, his dad needed a helicopter to visit the far ranges. Garrick had come east for his education and flew for the hospital's night shift.

Jeff had settled into an easygoing friendship with the sky jockey. Sometimes they double-dated; more often just the two of them sailed or water-skied without female company. After the intensity of the hospital, Jeff enjoyed a change from the usual medically related conversations of his colleagues.

"Actually I've got a date tonight," Jeff admitted, knowing Garrick wouldn't mind his cancellation of their tentative plans to go bowling.

"Anyone I know?"

"Chelsea came in by EMS. She has amnesia."

Garrick stopped chewing. "Has her memory returned?"

"Not yet."

Garrick rolled his eyes toward the ceiling. "You sure can pick 'em."

"What's that supposed to mean?"

"I thought the residents were supposed to give you interns enough to do, taking care of your patients in the hospital. *In,* being the operative word here. Must you follow the pretty ones home to be sure they're all right, too?"

"You got me. She is pretty." Jeff laughed and dug into his Caesar salad. "But Chelsea's strong."

Garrick shook his head, his lip curving into a grin. "Are you telling me she's lost her memory and she's not vulnerable? No way. I should take you for a ride over the city," Garrick teased. "Maybe the altitude would clear your head."

"You know I don't like heights."

"How can you be afraid of a little fresh air when you don't mind working up to your elbows in blood and guts?"

"Only you could compare a rational fear with saving a life."

Whenever Garrick suggested a helicopter ride, Jeff regretted telling him about the time another kid had dared him to jump off the railroad trestle into the river. When Jeff had refused to jump from the bridge, someone had pushed him. And he'd never forgotten that swooping, sickening fall before he smacked water hard as concrete. Sometimes he suspected Garrick made the offer to enjoy watching him squirm.

"Flying my chopper is not like falling off a bridge," Garrick insisted. "You're strapped in. There's machinery around you."

"I'll stay on the ground, thank you very much." Although Jeff reluctantly flew in airplanes, the mere thought of only a plastic bubble between him and thousands of feet of empty space made him break into a sweat.

"Chelsea might find a helicopter ride romantic."

Romance would have to wait until he was sure she was safe. Holding back last night had been a form of torture. After that one chaste brush of his lips against hers, it had taken all his control not to deepen the kiss. But he'd read the alarm in her gaze and recognized he'd lose her unless he went slowly. He wondered if she knew he'd barely slept. While he'd tossed and turned, imagining what it would be like to really kiss her, she must have slept soundly in her bed. Because despite her worries, her skin practically glowed over breakfast. Focusing on her problems was the only way he'd managed to resist sweeping her into his arms.

And this morning he'd already picked up the phone three times to call her but hung up instead. Sensing that his lengthy silence revealed more than he wished to his friend, Jeff explained, "We haven't gotten to romance yet."

"Sure." A wide smile creased Garrick's face. "That's why you came to work today wearing the same clothes you went home in last night."

Jeff frowned. "You were off yesterday. How could you possibly know what I was wearing?"

"I flew in an accident victim this morning. The nurses—"

"The nurses." Gossip spread faster than a virus in this place.

"So let me get this straight." Garrick pushed back his chair and sipped his iced tea. "You spent the night, didn't even score and you're asking her out again tonight. What gives?"

Jeff shrugged, reluctant to explain that Chelsea thought someone had tried to kill her and that she might be in danger. It just sounded too far out to be possible. "Why are you so interested?"

Refusing to be sidetracked, Garrick ignored Jeff's question and persisted. "Have you explained to her your I'm-not-going-to-get-married-ever attitude?"

Jeff winced at Garrick's sarcasm. "Chelsea has amnesia. She's more interested in finding out about her past than planning her future."

"Right."

"I'm just helping out."

"Right."

"So I like her a lot. No big deal."

"I assure you flying with me is much safer than falling in love."

"Cynic. Besides, you're getting ahead of yourself here. I slept in her guest room."

"Exactly. If you got a little and wanted more, I wouldn't be worried." Garrick's blue-black eyes twinkled. "But you're going back for more anyway."

Garrick rarely pressed. Clearly he suspected Jeff was holding out on him. Finally he changed the subject but still got in a last dig. "You know the nurses say the only way to get a doctor to make a house call is to marry him, don't you?"

Jeff's beeper went off, saving him from a reply. "It's from ICU. Gotta go."

As he hurried to the elevator that would shuttle him to ICU, Jeff could no longer deny that his interest in Chelsea was not simply doctor-patient. He liked Chelsea as a person. Who was he kidding—he more than liked her. Every time his gaze met hers, his heart fibrillated against his ribs, his pulse skyrocketed and he felt an overwhelming need to be close to her. She was disturbing to him in every way, physically and mentally.

He admired the strength with which she dealt with her amnesia. He'd kept expecting her to fall apart, but she never had.

And as fate tossed each challenge at her—the arrival of a baby she didn't know how to take care of, plus the possible attack followed by the threats—she hadn't flinched from her responsibility to Alex.

He admired her loyalty to a friend she couldn't remember. Approved of the way she'd taken custody of a child she didn't know. And perceptive guy that the pilot was, Garrick must have sensed Jeff's fascination with Chelsea Connors.

Jeff could have made excuses for his interest and told Garrick that she'd needed help with the baby. He could have mentioned the threatening phone call. But he'd jump at even a flimsy excuse to be with her again.

The way she'd taken to the baby appealed to him. She'd been unable to hide her worry when Alex wouldn't stop crying. Obviously the baby had already touched a place in her heart.

*Fast work, tiger.* Could he do as well?

Jeff stepped out of the elevator into ICU. Was Garrick right that he wanted a part of Chelsea for himself? He'd been anxious all morning, wondering about her day, her appointment, and he couldn't rationalize the worry away. He had this hunch that leaving Chelsea alone had been a mistake.

BACK AT CHELSEA'S OFFICE, shortly after lunch, the phone rang.

"It's Dr. Jeffrey Kendall," Sandy told her over the intercom. "You want to take it?"

"Sure." Chelsea punched a button, surprised at how eager she was to hear his voice. "Hello."

"How's it going?"

Excited that he'd called for seemingly no more reason than to talk about trivialities, she told him about her day. "Not much. I took a cab, stopped at the bank for some cash and shopped for diapers and formula. The trip tired Alex out."

"Are you managing okay?"

She grinned, proud that she was doing so well, pleased that he cared. "Alex is napping in his stroller in my office corner. But you should have heard him screaming during Officer Russo's call."

"What did he want?" Although Jeff's tone remained casual, she sensed he was now more alert.

"He asked how I was doing. But I suspect he was really checking to see if my memory's returned."

"Don't try to force it. It'll come." The warmth in his tone reassured her more than his words of encouragement.

"Russo did mention my car's still parked in front of Anne's house. He thinks I was probably in the process of moving the baby's boxes when I fell."

"You sound as if you don't believe him."

"I don't know what to think." Unsure whom to trust or what she should know, she was glad Jeff wanted to be her friend. She imagined him in his sexy blue scrubs and hoped they could be a lot more than friends. But that would have to wait until she learned more about her past.

"After dinner we'll pick up your car. I don't want you going back there alone."

"Thanks."

She hung up the phone, more than appreciative of his offer. And not just because she enjoyed Jeff's company. Returning to the house where Anne had been murdered, where Chelsea's own "accident" had occurred, left her uneasy. She couldn't explain the dread that overcame her but likened her apprehension to a horror movie where the victim walked down the steps into a darkened basement, scary music played, and one just knew something bad would happen. At least Jeff had agreed to go with her.

But before she met with Jeff, she had a good afternoon of work ahead of her. She needed Sandy to bring her up to speed on Classy Creations' personnel and finances. Maybe she'd find a clue to who wanted her dead.

She parked the stroller by her office window, where she could keep watch over Alex. She sat, overlooking the courtyard, on one of a pair of Georgian mahogany library armchairs with a padded back, armrests and seat. Sandy sat fidgeting in the matching chair.

"Sandy, I need your help to fill in the gaps. Did I build this firm from scratch?"

"You inherited Classy Creations and the house you live in from your uncle three years ago."

Chelsea couldn't recall the man's name or face. She experienced no sorrow for a stranger she couldn't remember. "Were we close?"

"I don't know. After he died in his sleep, you took over the firm."

"Did I work here before then?"

Sandy nodded, her gaze flitting about the room like a fly searching for a safe place to land. "As an assistant account executive."

So, due to her inheritance, Chelsea had jumped from assistant to company president. Could someone resent her inheritance or her sudden change in status at the firm? Judging from the state of her finances, she'd not done such a good job of running Classy Creations. Recalling her lavishly decorated home, she wondered if she'd sucked too much cash from the firm's operating capital. "Did I run the business into the ground? Why are we almost bankrupt?"

"Your uncle had been content with the small bread-and-butter accounts, local car dealers, the neighborhood real-estate franchises. You went after bigger clients."

"And?"

Sandy stared at her tea, avoiding her gaze. After a long pause, she picked up her cup and saucer from the table, rubbed the table free of nonexistent rings and spoke carefully. "You won some and lost some."

"I don't understand. Surely the success of a firm this size doesn't depend on one assistant account executive boosted to the presidency?"

"Last year you pulled everyone off the small accounts to work on your pitch to TRH." A hint of resentment entered Sandy's tone.

Chelsea's business decision shouldn't have caused such strong discontent in a secretary. She filed the thought away for future reference.

TRH was a huge conglomerate that encompassed everything from food products to farm equipment to the latest in computer technology. "And we didn't land TRH?"

"We won the contract...but we underbid. It's been a loss leader. A prestigious one, but we are in desperate need of cash to continue operations."

"And my vice president, Martin Tinsdale? What did he have to say about this huge commitment to TRH?"

Sandy's voice dropped to a whisper. "He disagreed with you."

"And?"

"You fired him." Sandy's lips compressed to a tight line of disapproval. Her tea sloshed into her saucer.

Was Chelsea an ogre? Or was the issue clouded by her possibly biased secretary? "Sandy, tell me I didn't fire the man only for disagreeing with me?"

"There were many disagreements."

The telephone threat echoed in her memory. Maybe her ex-vice president thought she owed him. Maybe she took exception to her inheritance and subsequent promotion to owner. Had Chelsea found her enemy?

The firm's former vice president must have resented being fired by a former account assistant. "Where is Martin Tinsdale now?"

Sandy placed the saucer on the end table, picked up the cup and placed a napkin in the spilled tea. "He's fifty-five years old. At his age, he's had difficulty finding another job."

Martin Tinsdale was still on Chelsea's mind when she strapped Alex into the back seat of the cab at the end of a long day. Sandy had given her a rundown on each employee, but from her temperamental art director, Mick, to her in-house accountant, Walter Brund, to the lowly copy editor, Vanessa Wells, the girl she'd met on the way to the elevator, no one seemed to have a motive to dislike her as much as Martin Tinsdale.

Except maybe the Carpenters. She needed to find out more about Anne's stepsister. She or her husband could have made the threatening call last night.

A small shudder crept down her back. How many enemies would crawl out of the woodwork of her past?

The cab took a corner, bringing her thoughts to more-immediate concerns. Chelsea glanced over her shoulder. The same gray Toyota that had been parked in front of her office building seemed to be following them. In the fading light of dusk and the heavy traffic, she couldn't be sure, but the hairs on her nape prickled.

She'd intended to ride home, shower and change before meeting Jeff. But going home, alone, to her empty house had lost all appeal. In fact, as the Toyota passed a car and slipped directly behind the cab, the idea of returning to her isolated house sent a chill down her spine.

"Driver," she called to the front of the cab, her gaze darting back to the Toyota, "do you think that car is following us?"

"Which car, lady?"

"The Toyota."

"Don't know. If you're mixed up in any funny business, I don't want to be involved. How about you get out here?"

Lord, that's all she needed. For the driver to strand her with the baby along the interstate in the middle of nowhere.

Although her heart beat a staccato, she forced herself to sound calm. "I must have been mistaken. But look, I'm running late. I need to go directly to the Crab Café."

The cab pulled a U-turn at the next intersection.

So did the Toyota.

# Chapter Six

*She'd escaped again.*

Chelsea Connors may have survived a blow to her head and the attack with a hypodermic, but she wouldn't be as lucky this time. Restless hands polished the toaster until it gleamed as bright as the freshly washed floor, then moved on to scrape a trace of grease from the stove.

The superior little bitch hadn't been alone with the baby last night. But she couldn't have slept well after hearing the threatening whisper. If she only knew the plan, she'd savor these waking hours—her last.

Like the dirt that must be vanquished, Chelsea Connors must die—tonight, before she regained her memories and recalled what she had seen.

Soon she would sleep.

Forever.

CHELSEA HURRIEDLY PAID and tipped the driver before he slowed in front of the trendy restaurant. Strains from a jazz band floated outside. The scrumptious scent of fresh-baked bread and grilled seafood would have whetted her appetite if she hadn't been so upset with whether the Toyota still followed her.

Eyes darting, she surveyed the restaurant, noting it attracted couples rather than a singles crowd. She waited for a chatting group of people to stroll from the parking lot to the café's sidewalk before exiting the cab, converting the car seat back to a stroller and trying to lose herself among them. She pushed Alex briskly through the double doors without looking back.

Already crowded, the restaurant was filled with couples, the casual drinkers on the back patio and the more serious ones bellying up to the polished art-deco bar inside.

Glancing at her watch, she realized it was only six-twenty. She couldn't expect Jeff to arrive until seven. But she should be safe amid so many people. And she should have time to feed Alex before dinner.

Chelsea asked for a rear booth in the nonsmoking section and informed the hostess that the other member of her party had yet to arrive. She saw no one suspicious and glanced down at Alex. He'd been so little trouble today, but she knew she couldn't count on him to always be so well behaved.

The hostess indicated a booth in a corner, and Chelsea converted the stroller back to a baby seat, lifted Alex onto it and scooted in beside him.

"You've been such a good boy," she crooned.

She needed to make child-care arrangements. And yet she didn't feel it would be safe to leave him when she suspected the Carpenters might have been behind the phone call last night. Horror numbed her at the possibility the baby might be what the caller had threatened to collect. The thought of losing Alex wrenched at her until she had to force her shoulders to relax.

"I'm going to take good care of you," she promised the baby.

She'd never know if it was the dim, multicolored overhead lighting, the sound of her voice or intestinal gas, but Alex smiled, his dimples deepening in his cherubic face. He gurgled and waved his chubby arms, and she stared at him with fascination, barely noticing the muted conversations or movements around her.

"Oh, you gorgeous little boy. When you grow up, I'm going to have to chase the girls away."

A deep, rich chuckle sounded by her ear, and she looked up, startled. When she recognized Jeff and his laughter, a warm glow encapsulated her.

"Hi." Jeff planted a kiss on her brow.

"You're early." She inhaled bay rum cologne and drank in the feeling of safety at his nearness.

Yet there was nothing safe about the cocky gleam in Jeff's bold glance. He took the seat across from her and ordered drinks, looking more handsome than he had a right to after what she assumed was a long, trying day at the hospital. He'd found time to change his clothes. The casual maroon V-necked sweater over a matching shirt contrasted with the teal of his sparkling eyes.

And suddenly the thought of the Toyota following her faded like yesterday's nightmare. Deciding not to say anything that she couldn't prove, especially since Jeff didn't believe someone had tried to kill her at the hospital, she lifted Alex out of his seat with a grin. "Did you see Alex smile at me? And his dimples deepened."

"Dimples are an imperfection," Jeff said teasingly.

Praying for the strength to resist his virile appeal, at least until she regained her memories, she kidded him right back, yearning for more light moments like this. "How dare you tell me my child isn't perfect in every way."

Jeff held up his hands in surrender. "Okay. Alex is perfect."

"I'm glad you think so." She chuckled, removed the bottle of formula she'd warmed before leaving Classy Creations and popped it between Alex's eager lips. "I love the soft feel of his skin and the awkward way he tries to hold the bottle between his fists."

"You sound like a woman in love."

"And how does a woman in love sound?"

"Happy. Excited. Obsessed."

*Obsessed.* She recalled the word from her appointment book. Had she been obsessed about her work before amnesia took her memory? Everything she'd learned indicated the business was her life. Odd that she hadn't wanted more. She jerked her head up. As their gazes locked over the candlelit table, she thought maybe she was due for a change. "Am I ignoring you?"

"No need to apologize." His murmur rippled through her like warm honey, inflamed her like fine wine. "I like watching the curl of your lip when you hold Alex."

Her voice raised half an octave in surprise. "I curl my lip?"

"The left corner rises, and then you pucker it in a cute half smile. And your eyes kind of glaze with a happy sheen."

"What a fanciful imagination you have."

"I'm just observant."

Wondering what else he saw when he looked at her but afraid to ask, she couldn't hold the intensity of his gaze. And she had no idea what to say. Thankful for the baby, she turned her attention to Alex, fussing with a suspender strap that didn't need straightening.

Heat had risen to Chelsea's cheeks at his compliments. Finally she regained control of her tongue. "And how was your day?" she asked, attempting to change the subject.

With a shake of his head and a smile that said he knew exactly what she was trying to do, he shook a finger at her. "Oh, no, you don't. All day I've looked forward to hearing what you've learned about yourself."

She frowned as she recalled Vanessa, the redheaded young woman she'd met at the elevator. Vanessa had clearly avoided looking at Chelsea. And then later, Sandy had been surprised when Chelsea had shared how her presentation was going. "It's not flattering."

"How's that?"

A waitress brought Jeff a glass of wine and a soft drink for her since she couldn't have alcohol so soon after her head injury. But Jeff didn't allow the short delay to keep him from pursuing his questions. "You found out you design ad campaigns for dirty politicians?"

She arched her brow. "My employees don't like me and probably with good reason."

"Oh, yes, I can see what a terrible person you are."

She shifted Alex to her shoulder and patted his back. Finding the soft sound of his burping into her ear oddly comforting, she snuggled him closer. "I fired a man for disagreeing with me."

His blue eyes glinted with wry amusement. "That's terrible."

"My rash decisions have driven the firm to a precarious position."

He stared at her over the rim of his glass, and his lips twitched. "You mean to tell me there's a woman of daring behind that demure pose?"

Strange how he saw her cool on the outside, wild on the inside. She saw herself as a pretender trying to fill a role and afraid of failure. "If you call 'daring' throwing away bread-and-butter accounts on a foolish dream, then I guess I'm daring. Although others might call it sheer stupidity."

"And who told you all this?"

"My secretary filled me in. The accountant, Walter, confirmed it."

"And this Walter, do you trust him?"

With one fingertip, Chelsea toyed with the beads of condensation on her glass. "Walter doesn't look like an accountant. He's at least six foot six and built like an NFL linebacker. During the entire time I spoke with him, he seemed uncomfortable, as if I were about to jump down his throat for giving me bad news. Or maybe as if he was hiding something, I couldn't tell."

"Some bosses do take out their frustrations on the messenger."

"I pulled Walter's file and reviewed his employee record. He was fired from his last job." She sighed and moved the baby to a sitting position on her lap. Each revelation added to her growing list of questions. "I wish I knew why I hired him."

"He's probably competent. Or maybe it's the soft side of your heart that you don't want to believe exists." Jeff held out his arms toward Alex. "Can I hold him?"

"Sure." She handed the baby across the table. Maybe she was being too hard on herself and only looking for the bad things, the not-so-nice parts of her character. She'd absorbed enough advertising studies to know that even beautiful women obsessed about what they considered ugly ears or saddlebag thighs. Was she doing the same thing about her past?

She leaned forward, elbows on the table, and rested her chin in her hands. "Being objective isn't easy."

"Not even when you have your memories," he reminded her gently, a bright flare of desire springing into his eyes. His soft tone sent shivers down her arms. Sensing the arousal behind his softly murmured words, she imagined what it would be like to have him talk to her in that intoxicating voice when he made love, imagined a golden flow of passion spiraling into raw, sensuous desire. Fire spread to her heart, and she forced herself to stop fantasizing. Ducking her head to avoid his gaze, she reminded herself that until she regained her memories, her life might not be her own to share.

As if deliberately breaking the sudden tension between them, Jeff fixed his attention on Alex. He reached into his jacket and when he pulled a furry, blue-white ghost with enormous black eyes and a pink tongue over his hand, Alex glued his gaze to it with seeming fascination.

Jeff wiggled his hand, opening and closing the puppet's mouth. A fleeting thought of his hands on her skin flitted through her mind before she ruthlessly pushed it away.

Jeff raised his voice two octaves to a squeak. "Hi, little tiger, my name is Jasper. I want to be your friend."

Alex grinned, and so did Chelsea. There was just something endearing about a man willing to make silly sounds and faces to win a smile from a baby. But seductive, not endearing, was the word she'd use to describe the way he made her flood with desire with just a look or a movement of his hand. She had to regain control of herself and was grateful Jeff could carry the conversation by himself.

"What did you say, tiger? Oh, yes. We have a present for your mama, too."

Jeff, the puppet still on his hand, reached beside him on the seat. In the dim light, he grinned and lifted a basket in sight. Earlier she'd been so absorbed with Alex's smile, Jeff had sneaked the basket by her.

"You brought me a stuffed animal?" The black-and-white, floppy-eared bundle made her fingers itch to stroke it. She recalled stating in the hospital that she didn't even have a dog, and she forced back tears at his thoughtfulness. His compassion and his sexy manner wrapped in one captivating package were more than any woman should have to resist unwrapping.

"There's a real puppy coming soon. My sister's dog is whelping." He held out the basket. "Here, want to hold her?"

What she wanted was to hold him. Instead, she took the basket, and their fingers grazed, transmitting a burning sweetness up her arm. She forced her tone to sound normal. "Will it be safe to keep a puppy around Alex?"

He laughed, his eyes crinkling at the corners. "In a few months, Alex will be crawling. It's the pup who'll be afraid of *him*."

She shrugged, feeling silly but happy that he was planning to see her in a month or two. A lot could happen in a short time. She could regain her memories. Find out what it felt like to run her hands through his thick hair. Find out if his kisses were as seductive as the heated promise in his eyes.

Despite her wayward thoughts, she tried to remain calm. "I'd like a female if there's one in the litter."

"I'll put a female on reserve," he said with a wickedly delightful grin.

They ate a wonderful crab dinner, lingered over coffee and then Jeff renewed his offer to drive her to Anne's house to retrieve her car.

Most homes in the neighborhood had their lights on at nine-thirty. But after the police officer had told her the house was vacant, Chelsea was surprised to see the light from a television screen shining through the window of the home of her former friend.

She exited the car and stared at the low-slung house where Anne had lived with her son. The small building didn't look any more familiar than her own home. She didn't recognize the stucco or the iron-railed front stoop or the worn-out shingles on the patched roof. And yet uneasiness stomped down her throat until she gasped for breath.

"What is it?" Jeff carried the sleeping baby over his shoulder. "What's wrong?"

"I don't know. It's like a memory on the tip of my tongue but just out of reach. I feel as if someone is looking at me, but when I turn around, no one's there."

Drawn forward like a marionette, she walked through air suddenly as thick as pea soup. Her hand shook as she pointed to the bottom of the steps. "That's where the neighbors found me."

The front door crashed open. Chelsea jumped back and let out a gasp.

A couple bulldozed out the front door as if pushed from behind. The woman, about forty-five, advanced with quick, no-nonsense steps. Her birdlike eyes focused on Alex with laser intensity. "There he is!"

Head bowed, her husband shuffled three paces behind, the jowls on his face quivering beneath a graying mustache. He patted her shoulder. "Honey, please don't cause—"

"Don't you *honey* me." She shrugged off his touch. "I'm not leaving until I get what I came for." The lady's nose twitched as she marched down on them. "I'm Mary Carpenter, and this is my husband, Tom."

"I'm Dr. Jeffrey Kendall and this is Chelsea Connors," Jeff introduced himself with a step forward, placing himself between the couple and Chelsea.

Chelsea couldn't remember ever meeting these people, but their names from her conversation with her attorney were familiar. As she recalled this couple wanted to take Alex from her, she chewed her bottom lip. From the moment Mary Carpenter had barged out the front door, she seemed on the attack. But would this ordinary-looking middle-aged couple go so far as to attempt to murder her to claim Alex?

Mary, her face drawn into sharp features by the tight bun knotted at the back of her head, peered around Jeff. "The woman from foster care told us you might bring Alex here when you came to get his things.

A healthy child has no business returning to the scene of his mother's murder. It could upset his constitution and make him sick.''

"Now, honey—"

"Hush, Tom.'' Mary peered through thick glasses at the doctor. "He *is* healthy, isn't he?''

"And how could that possibly be your concern?'' Jeff asked while Chelsea threw him a grateful glance and fought down swirling anxiety.

Mary clucked her tongue against the roof of her mouth and shook her head. "*We* are the only family this orphan has. So I'll thank you to hand him over.''

"No!'' Chelsea shouted, surprising herself by the violent feelings raging through her.

Mary Carpenter looked down her long nose as if Chelsea were lower than a worm. "Ah, so you *can* talk?''

It seemed impossible that in just a day, Chelsea had formed a bond with the baby, and yet her arms ached to hold him again. The fact that she didn't know how to raise a child didn't matter. No one was born knowing these things, and she would learn whatever was necessary.

Besides, Alex was alone and vulnerable, a situation with which Chelsea could empathize. If she hadn't been determined to keep the baby before she met this dried-up prune, she was more than determined now.

"No,'' she repeated. "You can't have him.''

At her shrill protest, three pairs of questioning eyes stared at Chelsea. The baby let out a soft cry, and Jeff handed Alex to her and draped his arm over her shoulder. The little body snuggled against her trustingly, and she vowed not to let him down.

Drawing a deep breath to calm her overwrought nerves, Chelsea gathered her courage and went on the offensive. Every protective instinct bucked to the surface, giving her tone a bitter-harsh kick. "And how are *you* related to my son?"

As if about to do battle, Mary drew herself to her full five-foot height. "I am Anne's stepsister, the child's aunt."

"Stepaunt," Chelsea interjected, unwilling to give an inch.

"And her only family."

"Honey—"

"And I told you to hush." Mary didn't spare a glance at Tom, but her low opinion of her husband was obvious by the sneer in her tone.

Chelsea shook her head to clear it of the eerie thought that someone or something lurked behind her, ready to attack. "Anne specified in her will that she wanted me to raise Alex."

"Anne didn't have enough sense to know what was good for her child. Be that as it may," Mary said stiffly.

The words echoed in Chelsea's head. *Be that as it may.* Who talked like that? Mary Carpenter might be in her forties but she spoke and acted as if she'd come from the previous century. No way could Chelsea imagine a child growing happily to adulthood in the Carpenters' home.

Mary spoke slowly, as if choosing her words with care. "Anne was not in her right mind those last few months. We came here to search for another will."

Chelsea's heart leapt and lodged in her throat. Only Jeff's gentle squeeze of warning kept her from shouting. "Did you find one?"

"No," Tom admitted.

Mary's chin jutted. "A judge will invalidate the existing will."

If the Carpenters intended to go to court and contest custody, she should try to find out more. Digging for information, she asked, "What do you mean, Anne wasn't in her right mind?"

"After she became...with child, she changed jobs, lost touch with her old friends. She became secretive. Perhaps the shame of her pregnancy was too much for her to bear."

Jeff raised his brow. "Shame?"

"Anne wasn't married. I always knew she'd come to a bad end." Mary spoke callously, as if her stepsister had deserved to be murdered. "I told her she should give the baby to Tom and me to raise. At least the child would have a father. But Anne wouldn't listen."

Interesting that Mary Carpenter had wanted Alex before Anne's death. Chelsea would be willing to bet the Carpenters never expected Anne to leave Alex to Chelsea. And if they'd murdered Anne, surely they wouldn't hesitate to come after her.

Chelsea intended to do everything possible to prevent this woman from taking Alex from her. With a shudder, she wondered how strong a case the Carpenters would have. If only she could remember. Could Anne's peculiar behavior before she'd died invalidate her will? Fear that the Carpenters' family ties could influence a judge made the rich food she'd eaten congeal in her stomach.

Jeff must have picked up on her concern. "You aren't a blood relative?"

"No, but—"

Sensing Mary Carpenter's uncertainty, Chelsea pressed her advantage. "Do you have children of your own, Mrs. Carpenter?"

Tom lifted his head, eyes wincing in pain. "We were never so blessed."

"He has a low sperm count." Mary spit the accusation, as if it made him less a man. He lowered his head, apparently willing to take the blame for their childless state, but not before Chelsea spied rip-roaring rage in his eyes.

If Mary Carpenter continually humiliated her husband like this, it seemed possible the abuse could cause him to explode. Perhaps Tom's rage at his own inability to sire children had erupted in violence. His meek demeanor might be no more than a disguise for something more sinister.

A tiny shudder trembled through Chelsea. She stepped closer to Jeff, who spoke quietly in the tension-filled yard. "Why didn't you adopt?"

"We tried, but none of the children offered fit our standards. Can you imagine—they asked us to take a deaf child? What would our friends have thought?"

In just a few minutes, Chelsea had come to dislike the Carpenters. After that last statement, she knew Mary Carpenter was one contemptible woman.

Swallowing a rude comeback, she tried to keep her tone even, but the acid crept through. "And what will happen if Alex develops a hearing deficiency? Tell us, what would the neighbors think?"

Ignoring Chelsea's sarcasm, Mary sniffed. "Alex is perfect, isn't he?"

The baby's perfection was the first thing they'd agreed on since Mary Carpenter had barged out the door, but Chelsea wasn't about to admit it. Blithely she lied. "Oh, didn't you hear his sniffles? I believe my son might be coming down with a cold."

At her bold lie, Jeff emitted a choked grunt, and his unusually blue eyes danced with amusement.

Mary ignored Chelsea's words. Perhaps she hadn't heard them, too concerned with issuing her threat. "We've hired an attorney, but it would be easier if you'd just consent to our adopting the child."

Easier for whom? Not for Chelsea. Certainly not for Alex. Giving her sweet baby to this peculiar couple would turn her stomach.

Suspecting she'd drawn all the information from the Carpenters she could without revealing her amnesia, Chelsea leaned into Jeff's arm, appreciating his support, and ended the discussion. "I'm keeping Alex."

Even if Alex weren't the only person in the world who belonged to her, the only person besides Jeff who helped to keep the loneliness away, Chelsea would have refused to give him up. Anne must have had good reason for leaving her son with Chelsea; it wasn't a decision a mother made lightly.

Although Chelsea couldn't remember her friend, she intended to carry out her wishes. She'd keep the baby and raise him the best way she knew.

She'd already learned how pleasant holding Alex could be. Something about the baby's innocent blue eyes and rosy cheeks made him infinitely appealing. Chelsea wanted the chance to watch him crawl and say his first word. She wanted to straighten his tie the night of his senior prom, congratulate him on his first job, fuss over his children.

The Carpenters couldn't have him. It wouldn't happen. Alex deserved better. The baby deserved a caring mother, and that excluded the dried-up old biddy. While Alex should have a father, Tom, Mary's shifty-eyed husband, wasn't good enough for him.

"Whether you keep Alex or not will be decided by the courts," Mary Carpenter huffed. She grabbed her husband by the arm and towed him away without a backward glance.

With the woman's disappearance through the gate, Chelsea turned to Jeff and squeezed his hand in relief. A popping sound drew her gaze to the stoop. She hadn't realized they had an audience until she glanced to the front porch of the rental house.

A gray-haired woman, chewing and popping gum, frowned. "Can I help—?" Her eyes widened in recognition. "Oh, hi. It's Chelsea, isn't it? About time you returned to pick up the rest of the baby's things."

Could this be Anne's mother, Alex's grandmother? No, that couldn't be right. If Anne had close relatives, it was unlikely she would have left Alex to Chelsea.

Confusion caused Chelsea to stammer.

Apparently realizing her bewilderment and saving her from awkward explanations, Jeff held out his hand to the older woman. "I don't believe we've met. I'm Dr. Jeffrey Kendall, a friend of Chelsea's."

The woman wiped her palm on the back of her jeans and then shook his proffered hand. "Marilyn Charles, Anne's landlady. Unlike her nasty relatives—" she glanced toward the fence where the Carpenters had disappeared "—Anne was a polite young woman, and her checks came like clockwork on the first of the month."

"Glad you remember her so fondly," Chelsea mumbled under her breath.

Jeff reached over and squeezed her hand. "Easy."

"The Carpenters came to search the house for a new will, but I see they left empty-handed. Anne had more sense than to leave those two anything as valuable as a baby. A crying shame what happened here. This is a nice neighborhood." Marilyn turned to Chelsea. "When you were injured and the ambulance came back again, the neighbors started to say the house was cursed. Bad for business."

Chelsea lifted her brows. "How kind of you to inquire about my injury."

Marilyn paid Chelsea's sarcasm no mind. And Chelsea got hold of herself. The Carpenters' appearance and threats may have thrown her, but she couldn't miss this opportunity to find out more about Anne.

The landlady opened the front door and led them inside the sparkling-clean ranch house. Boxes, labeled with a black marker like the ones in Chelsea's front hallway, sat neatly packed in the den.

Jeff glanced from the boxes back to the two cars, gauging the volume. "Do you think they'll fit in both vehicles?"

"I hope so." Chelsea assessed the lot, surprised a baby needed so much paraphernalia. "Only I don't want you to have to drive all the way back to my place."

Marilyn jerked her thumb at Jeff. "Ain't that what ya brought him for?"

Before Chelsea could answer, the landlady resumed talking. "I need that stuff gone. I've got out-of-towners coming in to look the place over tomorrow. Hopefully they won't find out Anne was murdered in the kitchen until after I get a deposit. I tell you, once the police got done, this place was a mess."

The landlady must have finally realized how cold she sounded. At Chelsea's glare, she offered a weak apology. "Sorry about Anne. Didn't know her personal-like. But she was too good to die the way she did."

Ghoulishly Chelsea couldn't keep her gaze from fixing on the spotless gray linoleum. "How did she die?"

"Stabbed once in the ca-rot-id artery was what the police said. But she must have hurt her attacker. Can't tell by the look of things now, but I cleaned up a trail of blood out the back door that the police said was different from hers. Was only fair I kept the security deposit for all the extra work."

Chelsea stiffened at the woman's callousness. She was talking about murder as though Anne had left dirty dishes in the kitchen sink. She swayed on her feet and reached for Jeff, then steadied herself with a firm grip on his arm. "Let's get out of here."

After Jeff packed the boxes in both vehicles, Chelsea followed him to her house. Confronting the Carpenters and visiting the scene of her friend's death had left her hands shaking, her stomach in knots.

Perhaps she hadn't slipped on those front steps. Maybe she'd fainted. For some reason, the image of a shadowy figure lunging out at her wouldn't go away, and she wondered if her memory could be returning. Jeff had told her in the hospital that a frightful event may have caused her to forget. She recalled the awful creepy feeling as she'd stood in the yard and faced the Carpenters. Had she seen them before—right before she'd been attacked?

Was it too far a stretch of the imagination for her to believe that the person who'd killed her friend could now be coming after her, too? She'd lost her memories at Anne's house, been attacked at the hospital, received a threatening phone call and had perhaps been followed. What did all that mean? And had these incidents begun with her fall or months before?

She was letting her imagination get the best of her. All she knew for sure was that she'd hit her head, lost her memory and received a sinister call. The attack with the hypodermic in the hospital could have been a dream—though she didn't believe it. And she still wasn't positive anyone had followed her from work.

Her thoughts seemed to go around and around without reaching any meaningful conclusions, and her head was pounding when she finally pulled into her garage. Glad Jeff accompanied her and she didn't have to enter the house alone, she lifted Alex out of her car.

She'd intended to leave the boxes until morning, but Jeff returned for the cartons while she fed Alex and put him to bed in his room for the night. Sweet baby. She smoothed down his hair and covered him with a blanket before turning out his light.

Jeff was just piling the last box, label out, in the hallway. She squinted at the hurriedly scrawled lettering. "Do you suppose any of Anne's personal things are in those boxes?"

He dusted off his hands and turned to her. "Why?"

"I thought she might have a photo album that I could save for Alex. He's bound to be curious about his mother."

"And father."

"I wonder why Anne never married him?"

"Some men aren't the marrying type."

By his tone, Chelsea suspected he was no longer talking about Alex's father. The pleasant fantasies she'd entertained over dinner of ever making love with this man scudded away like a wispy cloud of promise on a windy day. Jeff's words couldn't have been any clearer. But still she swiveled her head with a little jolt of apprehension, needing to hear his explanation. "What are you saying?"

He raked his long fingers through dark hair. "Perhaps Anne never told the father she was pregnant. Or maybe she made up a name on the birth certificate because she didn't know who the real father was."

Chelsea sensed Jeff was backpedaling and faced him square on. "Some men don't want the responsibility of children. They don't want to be tied down."

He neither admitted nor denied her words but rubbed his brow with an index finger, turned toward the boxes and studied the labels. "I think one of them was marked with Anne's name." He kneeled. "Here it is."

He carried the box into the den and set it in front of the couch. Chelsea walked into the kitchen in search of scissors to cut the packaging tape, anxious for a moment alone. Had Jeff been trying to tell her he didn't want marriage or children? She wasn't sure.

But the thought that he might be warning her off before they'd gotten to know each other seemed sad. He'd told her almost nothing about himself. She'd like to find out more.

Grabbing the scissors with renewed determination, she headed straight to the carton. Her eagerness making her clumsy, she fumbled for a minute before he held out his hand. "Why don't you let me do that?"

"Thanks. I guess I'm nervous."

"Why? You look as composed as a high-fashion model."

The ring of the phone interrupted her reply. Rushing to the den, she worried if the anonymous caller would issue another threat. "Hello."

"Chelsea Connors?"

"Speaking."

"This is Detective Burdett." She didn't recognize the name. "I have a few more questions I'd like to ask concerning Anne's murder. Would you mind if I stopped by?"

Although she couldn't recall Burdett's name or face, she must have previously spoken to him about Anne's murder. "It's after eleven."

"Once we begin a murder investigation, we work twenty-four hours a day. I won't keep you long."

"Okay, but—"

"Thanks. See you in about ten minutes."

While she'd spoken, Jeff opened the carton. He hadn't looked inside but waited for her to finish her phone conversation.

"That was Detective Burdett. He wants to ask me some more questions. He hung up before I could explain about my amnesia."

"But maybe he can help you."

"What do you mean?"

"He'll have investigated Anne and your relationship with her. Maybe he can fill in some of your memory gaps."

"You're right." Jeff always seemed to know what to say to make her feel better.

"Let's see what's in the box. I'm assuming the police already went through her belongings and kept the interesting effects for evidence."

"Interesting effects?"

"Tax returns, bank statements, personal phone directories."

The contents of the box proved disappointing. A few pieces of costume jewelry, cosmetics, assorted articles of clothing and several romance novels with intriguing titles.

Chelsea looked up from the meager stack and wondered what she'd hoped to find. A letter explaining why Anne had left Alex to her best friend? A note naming her murderer?

At the bottom of the box was a photograph of a woman holding Alex, marked Mommy And Alex on the back. Chelsea immediately recognized Anne as the woman in her dream. Her face was happy but tired, and she held Alex with such a mixture of tenderness and pride, there could be no doubting her love.

She remembered Anne calling in her dream. *Promise me,* Anne had pleaded in a voice racked with agony.

Promise her what? Chelsea shook her head. Although only a dream, her first memory with a connection to her past puzzled her.

The doorbell rang, and while she packed Anne's belongings away, determined to save everything for Alex, Jeff answered the door. He returned with a tall, sharp-eyed man. "This is Detective Burdett."

"We've met." The detective greeted her without a smile. "I'm sorry to interrupt your evening, Ms. Connors."

"Chelsea," she insisted, having no memory of their previous meeting. "Please have a seat, Detective. Can I get you coffee or tea?"

"Coffee with cream would be great."

She fixed coffee in the kitchen while the men introduced themselves. When she returned with a tray, the officer sat straight in the lounge chair, his squared shoulders resisting the cushy leather. Jeff leaned back on the sofa, his long legs stretched out in front of him. Setting the tray on the table, she let the men help themselves while she took a seat beside Jeff.

As if sensing the interview would be difficult for her, Jeff took her hand and knit their fingers together, his warmth heating her icy fingers. Glad Jeff was beside her, she gazed back at the detective with a measure of calm she didn't feel.

The detective scowled, annoyance in his tone. "If you'd been straight with me the first time we spoke, you could have saved me three weeks of work. Why didn't you tell me Anne Spears changed her name and her job about a year ago?"

"I don't know," Chelsea said. "You see—"

"Why didn't you tell me that Albert Marcel Llewellyn is dead?"

"What?" Chelsea's bones felt as if they'd turned to water. Alex's father was dead. Although she felt guilty, relief stabbed her. The missing father couldn't show up and take Alex away.

The detective leaned forward, his hands on his thighs. "Nor could this Albert have been the baby's father."

He was going too fast. Just when she felt safe, he'd yanked the rug out from beneath her feet. She put down her coffee before she spilled it. "I have no idea what you're talking about."

"There aren't many Albert Marcel Llewellyns in Maryland. I checked them all. You know how many I found?" He answered his own question. "One."

"So what's the problem?" Jeff asked.

Burdett thrust his chin forward. "Six months ago, Albert died. He was ninety-seven years old, and he spent the last five years in bed in a nursing home. Somehow I don't think he fathered Alex. And I want to know who did."

Stunned, Chelsea fought to keep her voice steady. "I don't know."

Burdett's anger lashed at her like a whip. "Anne was your best friend, and she never told you she picked a dead man's name to put on the birth certificate? She never told you why she was on the run, why she changed her name, moved and switched jobs?"

"If she did, I don't remember. I—"

"Young lady, you do realize your friend was murdered?"

"If you'd just let me—"

"You realize withholding evidence in a criminal investigation is a crime?"

Jeff slapped the coffee table with his palm. His voice hardened to steel. "That's enough. Chelsea has suffered from amnesia ever since her accident when she went to retrieve the baby's belongings. If you don't believe me, her doctor, an Officer Russo filled out a report at the hospital which will confirm my statement. Chelsea can't help you because she cannot remember. So stop badgering her."

Burdett's lower jaw fell open. "I apologize, ma'am. Why didn't you explain in the first place?"

At the detective's complete attitude adjustment from snarling pit bull to meek pussycat, she had to restrain her grin. "You didn't give me a chance. But I want to find Anne's murderer as much as you do. If or when my memory returns, I'll be sure to call you."

After Burdett left, Jeff sat with Chelsea on the couch. She wanted to rest her head against his shoulder, to snuggle against his firm strength, but couldn't find the courage to close the distance between them. Her pulse skittered alarmingly. "Thank you for rescuing me."

His eyes smoldered, but whether from his annoyance with Burdett or in response to her proximity she wasn't sure. "I only let him go on as long as I did because he was giving us so much information."

He moved, his thigh barely touching hers. Heat ran down her leg, up her stomach, curled in her heart. Her body felt as if half ice, half flame. Surely her feelings couldn't be one-sided? With a soft sigh, she leaned closer to him, keenly aware of the wistfulness stealing over her expression.

He smoothed her bangs off her forehead, tracing her stitches with a gentle finger that almost snapped her patience. "You look like a cat that just lapped the last of the cream. What are you thinking?"

"About how compatible we are." The prolonged anticipation was almost unbearable. Didn't the man want to kiss her? Surely he knew what effect his proximity was having on her. Her impatience grew. Surely no one could be so completely unaware of his own sexual appeal.

As if holding a raw emotion in check, he merely raised a brow. "Oh?"

Momentarily rebuffed, she concealed her inner turmoil. But damn him! He'd discuss this to death before getting around to kissing her. She babbled an explanation as she fought swirling desire. "You see, I also wanted to hear the rest of the information about Anne. I may have amnesia, but I'm fully capable of stopping a cop from harassing me." She tilted her head to meet the maddening but dizzying magnetism in his gaze that she was powerless to resist. "But it was most chivalrous of you to jump in and protect me."

With her lips just inches from his, her invitation couldn't have been any clearer. And he didn't disappoint her. As if knowing she couldn't wait another moment, slowly, ever so slowly, he tilted his head and nibbled her lips. She slipped her arms around his neck and twined her fingers into his hair. Tasting of coffee, he deepened the kiss.

His carnal pull was ardent, arousing, turbulent. She felt as if she'd taken a ride on a roller coaster without a safety harness and was about to spin upside down. Her lungs starved for air, and her heart pumped erratically.

Breathless, she drew back, her eyes staring into his, wondering what she meant to him. And what did he mean to her? His knuckles grazed her cheek. This was not just lust. She enjoyed his conversations, his company, his support.

And yet deepening their relationship before her memory returned would be wrong. With the roller-coaster ride he'd taken her on at a complete halt, she felt suspended in midair and about to swoop out of control.

Filled with a warm, heady flush of desire from his kiss, she reluctantly stood and placed the coffee cups and saucers on the tray. Glancing out the front window, she noted a car driving slowly by, but her thoughts focused on that heart-stopping kiss and her wildly responsive reaction.

From the back bedroom, Alex let out a cry. She stopped abruptly to listen to determine if he was really awake, the cups on the tray clattering as she froze.

The shot blasted through the window like a bomb at ground zero. Glass shattered and sprayed from the window. The tray flew from her hands. And Chelsea dropped to the floor.

# Chapter Seven

In that split second, Jeff lunged from the couch and pinned Chelsea to the floor, covering her with his body. "Stay down."

Several additional shots slammed into the room, and terror paralyzed her, rising in her throat to choke her. Stopping to listen for Alex's cry had probably saved her life. Outside, tires squealed as if to make a quick getaway.

Alex screamed.

*No. Not the baby.* Ignoring her galloping fear for her own safety, she struggled beneath Jeff's crushing weight, her breath hissing. A damned fine time for his protective instincts to kick in. "Let me up!"

"Wait."

She couldn't let anything happen to Alex. An edge of panic made her tone shrill. "I have to go to the baby."

"The shots came from the street." Jeff spoke calmly, soothingly, as if he ducked bullets for a living. "Alex is in the rear bedroom. He'll be fine. If it weren't for the broken glass, we could crawl. Before we present a vertical target, let's be sure that no one's coming back."

At his sensible precaution, she stopping struggling. As they lay together, waiting for another attack, their bodies pressed intimately enough for him to feel the pounding of her heart, she held back the howl of fear rising in her throat, held back the urge to dash to the baby in panic.

"Are you hurt?" he asked in a voice so calm she wanted to scream at him until he acknowledged the danger of their situation. While he might be accustomed to life-and-death circumstances, she definitely was not.

"I'm okay, except for maybe the bruised ribs you pounded into the floor." She had difficulty saying the words through a dust-dry mouth. And neither his weight nor his hard warmth stilled her trembling at having to face mortality. She could have been living and breathing one second, her blood and flesh plastered across the wall the next.

The baby's crying jolted her already shaken nerves. "If Alex hadn't cried out, I might have walked straight into a bullet." She had to stop thinking of death. "Are you hurt?"

"Never better. Sorry I didn't believe someone attacked you in the hospital."

"And I'm sorry I got you into this. Although what 'this' is about, I haven't a clue. Do you think we can stand now?"

"With the lights on, we make a natural target. Let's wait another minute. Alex's cry doesn't sound like he's in pain—just scared."

"How do you know?"

"After you've been around as many crying babies as I have, you develop an instinct."

She hoped his instincts were correct, because Alex's heartrending cries seemed to suck every atom of self-control from her body. If Jeff hadn't pinned her, she would have darted to the baby, heedless of danger.

The seconds ticked by slowly. When she drew in a breath, inhaled dust from the plaster stuck in her windpipe, she coughed. Alex kept screaming. Police sirens wailed, steadily growing in intensity, and Chelsea silently thanked some concerned neighbor for calling the police.

She should have used the time to regain control of herself, but Alex's screeching was like alcohol on a raw wound. She had to clench her fists to stop twitching in response to every cry.

When a cruiser pulled into the driveway, its blue lights flashing on the walls of her den, Jeff clambered to his feet. "Let me help you up. There's glass everywhere."

She scooted onto her side, and he extended his hand and tugged. Glass crunched and hastened her footsteps.

She left Jeff to talk to the cops. Urged on by Alex's cries, she pelted down the hall. With a damp palm, she opened his door and flicked on the light in the nursery, her gaze speeding to the crib.

The baby's face was red from crying, his eyes swollen. His chubby arms waved fiercely, but otherwise, he appeared unharmed, and the knots in her stomach loosened.

When Alex spotted her, his sharp cries softened to a whimper. Scooping him into her arms, she cradled him against her and rocked away his fears. "Mama's here, tiger. It's going to be okay. I won't let anyone hurt you."

The sound of her voice calmed Alex, and his tears disappeared. Quickly she changed his diaper, marveling at how proficient she'd become at the task in just a day. Even with her hands shaking and her knees weak, she had Alex ready in seconds.

After carrying him into the kitchen, she took a bottle from the fridge, unscrewed the nipple and placed it in the microwave. She didn't know if a feeding would calm *him,* but the need to hold him would soothe *her.* "Mama will heat you a midnight snack."

Two police officers, an Asian-American female and a white male, stood opposite the window by the living-room wall, prying bullets out of drywall. The woman, her short black hair glinting in the light, picked her way through the debris toward Chelsea in the kitchen. "Is anyone injured?"

"We're fine." Except for being frightened to death.

The woman had kind brown eyes and a worried frown on her thin lips. "Any idea who could have done this?"

"I don't know." Chelsea shoved her bangs off her face. "This is the second attempt on my life this week."

The female cop shot her a skeptical look. "So this isn't a random act of violence?"

"This may look like a drive-by shooting, but the target, *me,* was not arbitrary."

The policewoman scowled. "Someone's shot at you from the street before?"

The microwave beeped, and Chelsea removed the bottle, twisted off the cap, replaced the nipple and placed it between Alex's lips. At the kitchen table,

Chelsea scooted out a chair with her foot and sat. Jeff and the other police officer, a man with bulldog jowls and baby-faced skin, headed out the front door into the yard.

After the female officer made herself comfortable, Chelsea told her about the accident that caused her amnesia, the subsequent attack in the hospital, the threatening phone call and her suspicion of being followed.

"You sound positive someone is after you. Any idea who? Or perhaps you have some evidence, like a license tag?"

"Sorry." Chelsea shook her head, glad she had Alex to look after. Caring for him helped her keep herself together, helped keep her from snapping at the suspicious officer, who was just doing her job.

The officer pressed her. "Most murder attempts are committed by someone the victim knows—an ex-husband, a jealous lover."

*Stay calm, rational.* "As far as I know, I'm single. There's no evidence I've ever been married, but then again, I'm not certain. My past is pretty much a mystery. But—"

"Yes?"

"My phone number is unlisted, yet I've had that threatening phone call. That would mean whoever is after me either knows me or got the number from someone who knows me."

Jeff and the other officer entered the kitchen through the back door. While she'd been talking, they must have searched the yard.

Jeff folded his arms across his chest and leaned back against the counter. "You might want to inform Detective Burdett about this incident. He just left here and he's investigating the murder of the baby's mother.''

Chelsea cocked her head. Could there be a connection? The vivid dream about Anne she'd had in the hospital popped into her mind. She'd promised Alex's mother something and sighed with dissatisfaction that she was still unable to dredge up the conversation. Unfortunately, idle speculation would serve no useful purpose without hard facts to back it up.

While she fed Alex, Jeff answered most of the police questions with ''We don't know.''

Alex eventually shut his eyes and fell asleep. She put him to bed and returned to the front hall as the police were leaving, the dark-haired officer speaking to Jeff. ''We'll have a patrol car drive by more frequently. You're probably safe tonight. It's doubtful anyone will return to bother you so soon, especially with our extra patrols in force.''

''Thanks. Good night, officers. I'll stay with her.'' Jeff's offer was more statement than question. He closed the door and locked it, then grinned wryly, apparently realizing how futile locking the door was when anyone could climb in the gaping window. ''We'll have to wait until tomorrow to board up the hole. At least the nights are still warm.''

Ignoring her still-shaking hands, Chelsea grabbed a broom out of the pantry and began to sweep the glass into a pile.

Jeff picked up the bigger pieces and threw them in the trash. ''Do you think someone from Classy Creations fired that shot?''

Chelsea whipped her head around to look at him and swallowed down her fear. "I think whoever killed Anne may be after me."

At least Jeff didn't laugh at her supposition. Although from the skeptical gleam in his eyes, he appeared far from convinced of her leap in logic. "What makes you think there's a connection?"

She leaned on the broom handle, her thoughts swirling. "It's too much of a coincidence that my best friend is killed and now someone is after me for there *not* to be a connection."

He nodded cautiously. "Go on."

"Suppose the killer wanted something of Anne's but didn't get it? I inherited her possessions right down to Alex. So maybe now the killer has decided to come after me."

Jeff considered her line of reasoning without outright rejection. "Who would inherit *your* estate?"

Chelsea shrugged helplessly, knowing her logic fell apart at this point. "According to Sandy, until I received Classy Creations and this house from my uncle, I didn't have many assets. As far as I know, I never got around to making a will."

Jeff's glance roved down the hall toward the unpacked boxes. "Did Anne leave you anything valuable?"

"I think it's time to find out. And it might be time to turn this house upside down to search for any potential clues. Maybe I'll even find my missing gun."

Jeff opened the boxes in the hall and pawed through baby clothes. "Are there any other possible suspects from work, or someone who knew both you and Anne?"

She groaned but wanted to shout her frustration. "It's so hard—not remembering. I have trouble judging what I see. The smallest things could mean nothing or everything."

Jeff set aside the first box and started on another. "For example?"

"Sandy is an odd duck. She's always cleaning, polishing, scrubbing the office and feeding and watering the plants, but I have to admit she seems on top of everything."

"Cleaning isn't a crime."

"But she's always watching me, and I don't know if she normally does that, or if she's waiting for me to make mistakes or if she's watching for my memory to return." Chelsea sighed. "And Vanessa, my copy editor, won't look at me. But that may not be important."

"That's it?"

Chelsea dug into a carton. "There's the Carpenters, the couple that wants to take Alex from me. But they intend to go to court. Why risk murder if they can take Alex legally?"

Besides an antique set of chipped china, a few sterling pieces that needed polishing and a hand-painted doll in satin, they found nothing of value in the boxes of baby clothes, toys and linens.

And they had no further luck searching Chelsea's house, either. She found no private letters, no old newspaper clippings. In exhaustion she sat in the kitchen drinking black coffee and puzzling over her personal planner. But the initials swam before her eyes. She shoved it away in frustration and stalked into the den to finish cleaning the broken glass.

She swept angrily, her fingers wrapped tightly around the broom handle, rage fueling her. Why had she lost her memory at the time she needed it most? Damn. Her eyes grew hot with held-back tears. Her life might depend on the answers, and yet her mind refused to cooperate. Her hands trembled as the helplessness of her situation overwhelmed her.

Jeff followed her into the room and took the broom from her. "You're exhausted. This can wait until morning."

"I guess."

She swayed on her feet. Jeff's arms closed around her. She pressed her ear to his beating heart, wanting to stay exactly where she was—forever.

His voice spoke reassuringly in her ear. "I'm going to sleep beside you tonight. I want to hold you, nothing more, okay?"

*Liar.* Holding her felt so good, he didn't ever want to let her go. He inhaled the scent of her shampoo, mixed with the subtle smell of jasmine soap. She felt soft, fragile, and yet he'd seen her steely core when she'd refused to panic after almost dying. He wanted to do a lot more than hold her. Yet he'd be a cad to take advantage of her after all she'd been through.

Embracing her made him long to nibble a path along her neck, taste her lips, learn every inch of her flesh. With her breasts pressed tauntingly against him, his fingers hungered to slip beneath her blouse and his tongue yearned to taste her.

He shifted to prevent her feeling the growing hardness in his groin and bit back a groan. Spending the night beside her without making love would be sweet torture. But no matter how much he wanted more, he wouldn't miss the experience of holding her close.

Slinging his arm over her shoulder, he turned out the light and strolled with her toward her bedroom.

"Why are you so good to me?" she murmured. "I don't deserve you."

He halted in the hall. When she turned to him, he sensed her puzzlement. Flattening his palms on either side of her head, he backed her against the wall, his tone rough. "Don't ever say that again. You deserve the best, more than I can give you."

She raised her hand to trail her fingers along his cheekbone. "What is it you're afraid you can't give me?"

The question she'd asked mirrored the multitude of doubts in her eyes. But he didn't have answers for her. Not then. Maybe not ever.

"Come." He took her hand and, when she didn't pull away, took it as a positive sign. "You're exhausted. We can talk in the morning."

She didn't turn on the bedroom light but left him in the moonlit room to enter what he assumed was the bathroom. Returning a few minutes later, she remained fully dressed.

After pulling down the quilt, she lay stiffly on her back, her hands clasped behind her head. He remained at the window, staring out into the endless dark sky, wondering how many nights he was destined to spend alone. God, he wanted her.

"Come to bed and hold me like you promised, Doctor."

He didn't need a second invitation. After kicking off his shoes, he joined her, slipping his hand beneath her neck and drawing her against his side. He pressed his lips to her forehead and told himself to be satisfied that she trusted him to hold her. Only he hadn't known how difficult just holding her would be when his body demanded more.

He could seduce her. But he didn't want to betray her trust. So, like an idiot, he held her, pretending everything was fine when the sweet scent of her practically had him climbing the walls.

She snuggled with her head to his chest, her arm thrown over his waist. He smoothed her hair along her face, marveling at the silky tresses, the creamy softness of her skin. But as much as he ached to explore her body, from her full lips to her perky breasts to her little toes, he wouldn't risk her thinking badly of him.

"Jeff?"

"Yes."

"Earlier I think someone followed me from the office to the restaurant."

He stiffened, at first angry, then hurt she hadn't trusted him enough to voice her suspicions. "Why didn't you tell me before?"

"I had no proof, just like after the attack at the hospital." He hadn't believed her then. No wonder she didn't trust him. "I didn't want to come off as a nut case."

"Tomorrow I want you to pack and move into my house."

"We barely know each other."

"No strings, Chelsea. You can have a bedroom to yourself and so can Alex. You'll be safer with me than at a hotel. And I'll feel better keeping an eye on you. My house is private. Whoever is after you will have trouble finding you there."

"Am I supposed to hide forever?"

*Forever* had a nice solid ring to it until he reconsidered. He'd never wanted permanency before, never thought about it. But he forced himself to think, hoping it would curtail his raging desire. With the hectic schedule of a surgeon, there was no place in his life for a wife. He was the child of a surgeon. He knew well the price he and his family, especially his mother, had paid. The life he'd mapped had no room for family.

Yet he'd offered Chelsea his home without considering the future but thinking only of her safety. That was so unlike him he had to wonder why he'd made the offer. He tried to convince himself the attempt on her life must have shaken him more than he'd thought. But his excuse was lame.

"Stay, just until the police find this lunatic."

"I'll think about it. I do appreciate your offer. I'm just scared they won't ever make an arrest."

"They will."

"I'm scared my memory won't return—and scared that it will."

He tried to reassure her with concrete facts. "My property is set behind a fence, so another drive-by shooting will be impossible there. It's very private, woods surround the house, which backs up to the Chesapeake. Maybe you should take a few days off work."

Her hand drifted to his chest, the fingertips lightly exploring, and he wondered if she had any idea how her not-so-innocent touching sparked a flame of desire into a white-hot fire.

"I have to go in to work."

"All the money in the world won't do you good if you're six feet under."

She snuggled closer. "How comforting. You should have been a lawyer. You're very convincing."

"I never considered any career other than medicine." And that was why he couldn't have her.

"What about your sisters and brothers? Are any of them doctors?"

"Allison has a doctorate in history."

"And?"

Odd how she could read the pauses at the end of his sentences and urge him to fill the gaps. But at least talking helped take his mind off the fact he was lying in bed with a gorgeous woman and he wasn't doing anything to sate his needs. "My mother just applied and was accepted to medical school. She wants to work with Dad."

"That's terrific."

"I really admire her. She doesn't want to miss out on any part of life. She raised her family and now she wants a career."

"What does your dad think?"

He grinned in the darkness and caressed her hip. "He fusses if dinner isn't on the table when he comes home."

"Please don't tell me your mother is going to quit medical school to stay home and cook his dinner."

Jeff laughed. "Oh, no. She hired a cook."

"You sound like you approve."

"I do. They're happy."

She sighed at the pleasant picture he'd created. "I wish I could remember my family."

"Not every part of life is so good to remember."

"Like what?"

"I can't forget the years my mother spent alone. She tried to hide her sadness when Dad didn't show for things like their fifteenth wedding anniversary. She was brave attending every social function alone. But at night, sometimes I heard her crying."

"And you vowed not to have any woman crying over you?" she guessed, a small shudder going through her at the implication. He didn't want a wife in his life.

"Something like that." His fingers clenched around a lock of her hair.

"Do you think your mother would trade those spilled tears for a life without your father?"

He forced his fingers to uncurl. "I don't know."

"And what about you?" she pressed gently, hating the way he'd stiffened beside her but unable to alleviate his sadness. "Would you rather not be here at all? Do you remember your childhood fondly?"

"Of course I'm glad to be alive. Mom did a good job of raising us. We didn't want for anything, but Dad's attention. Kids from divorced families could say the same thing. But that doesn't mean divorce is desirable or it's fine for children to grow up without their fathers at home."

Chelsea couldn't argue with that. Actually she didn't want to argue at all.

After the long day, exhaustion overtook her. Snuggled with her head against Jeff's chest, she fell asleep. And dreamed of Anne.

Alex's mother pleaded with her. "Promise me!"

"I will," Chelsea replied.

"Promise me you'll do it for Alex's sake."

"It won't come to that."

"Do I have your word?" Anne pressed.

Chelsea threw up her hands in surrender. "I'll do it. I'll do it. I'll do it."

THE NEXT MORNING, Chelsea awakened from her dream, her legs twisted in the blankets, her arms sprawled over her pillow. The water ran in the shower, and the phone rang beside her bed.

Sleepily she picked up the receiver.

Her secretary's crisp voice cut through the fog that seemed to have invaded her brain. "It's Sandy. Aren't you coming in today?"

"We work on Saturday?"

"Until one o'clock. You always said it was your most productive day."

Chelsea rubbed the tiredness from her eyes and swung her legs over the side of the bed and sat. "I have to move today."

"Why?"

That someone wanted her dead still seemed unreal to her. Images from last night flashed in her mind, the sound of the shot, the flying glass, Jeff protecting her with his body. "Last night someone shot out my window."

Sandy gasped. "Are you okay?"

"Yes. But I think it might be better if I don't spend another night here. I'll give you my new phone number as soon as I get settled."

"Martin Tinsdale's wife has called four times to speak with you. She sounds desperate."

Of all her acquaintances, her former vice president had the best reason to hate her. Talking to his wife might be a good way to feel out the degree of his anger.

"You told me not to put her calls through," Sandy continued. "But since you don't remember... I thought you might want to know."

"You think I should talk to her?"

"It's your decision. But what harm can speaking with her do?"

"Okay, set an appointment for his wife next week. Have her bring Martin, too. Anything else?"

"I was saving the best news. Mark Lindstrom is ready to go ahead with the contract."

Chelsea raised a clenched fist into the air. "Yes!"

"He's insisting on signing this morning."

Chelsea rubbed her forehead. "Why the rush?"

Sandy sighed, no doubt tired of reminding her about things. "Benedict Academy's 150th-anniversary celebration is next weekend. You told Mr. Lindstrom it would be a good idea to invite the press and announce the new policy during the festivities."

"We'll need press releases faxed immediately."

"I'll take care of that this morning. But what about the contract?"

"Ask Mr. Lindstrom if he can meet me here. Explain that my front window was shot out, and I can't leave for the office right now. Unless I hear from you, I'll expect him between nine and ten."

"I'll get right on it."

"Anything else that can't wait until Monday?"

"I guess not."

"Make sure everyone from the firm is notified about the Benedict Academy party."

"Um."

"What is it?" Had Chelsea said something out of character again?

"You normally don't invite us."

"Everyone worked to land that account. We should all be involved in the celebration."

"But what if your memory returns before Friday night? People will have bought fancy dresses and made plans...."

"Even if my memory returns, I won't change my mind." Chelsea cradled the receiver, wondering what kind of person she'd been before and if she wanted to be that same person again. Cold. Ambitious. Alone, except for Anne.

Perhaps her dreams about Anne were a sign her memory was coming back and her subconscious was nagging her to recall something important. In her dream, Anne's voice had been fierce, almost hysterical, and yet Chelsea hadn't seen her friend's face again. Was Anne's message important? Or was it just a silly dream?

Padding down the hall to Alex, Chelsea peeked through the open door of his room. His crib was empty.

Jeff must have already changed and fed him. That man seemed to need very little sleep. As she made her way into the den and toward the playpen, she smiled at how easily she'd slept with him—as if they'd been longtime lovers.

Alex wasn't in the playpen, his high chair or his swing. Concern knit Chelsea's brows, and she hurried back to her bedroom, following the sound of Jeff's whistling.

He'd finished his shower and strode out of the bathroom with Alex wrapped in a towel in his arms. "He got a kick out of his shower."

Relief washed over her, and she felt a little silly for her concern. She walked to him and took Alex, wanting to reassure herself by holding him. "You took the baby in there with you?"

Jeff grinned, revealing even white teeth. "Sure. Alex didn't seem to mind the water dripping down his face. Do you think we should teach him to swim?"

Her houseguest wore only a towel wrapped around his waist. She raised her chin, trying not to look at all that bared golden skin on his chest, trying not to let the sight of him set her every nerve ending to tingling. "Alex is only three months old."

"A baby spends months inside the womb. Being in water is natural to him. I'd bet he'd take to swimming like a duck to water. I've got a whirlpool at my place."

Straightening her spine, she looked him straight in the eye. "Maybe we'll come visit."

"I want you to move in." His voice was husky in the morning. His wet hair glistened, drops of water spiked his long, dark lashes. Standing with nothing more than terry cloth about his lean hips, he looked like a Greek god not a doctor, and his appeal wasn't just devastating to her senses, but lethal to her heart.

And Lordy, he could be persuasive. "My house is safer than a hotel," he repeated the point from last night's argument. "Think of where the little guy will be better off. Besides, you should know by now I won't press you for intimacy."

She didn't fear pressure from him. Last night he'd shown he could be the perfect gentleman. No, she had nothing to fear from him—only herself and her constant attraction to him. She wanted to regain her memories before throwing herself into his arms, and his bed.

She thought about Jeff's offer while she showered, dressed and ate breakfast. By the time Mark Lindstrom arrived in a red Mustang, she was packed and they'd cleaned up the glass, but she was still undecided about whether to move to Jeff's house or settle into a hotel.

After answering the door, she led Mark down the hall into the kitchen. Alex sat in his swing, content to play with a large plastic ball. Jeff had gone to buy plywood to board up the window.

"Sorry to make you drive out here, but someone shot out my front window last night."

Mark studied the jagged break in the window, then removed his glasses from the bridge of his nose, unfolded a tiny square of tissue and began the ritual of cleaning his lenses. "Any idea who shot at you?"

"No. The police are working on it."

"Do they have any leads?"

She turned toward the counter, preferring to face the warmth of the kitchen rather than the reminder of last night's terror. "I'm not sure. Would you care for a cup of coffee?"

"No, thanks." Mark set his briefcase on the counter and unlocked it. "I took the liberty of making an extra copy so we could both have a signed version."

She hadn't thought of that. Her mind had been elsewhere, not focused on business. "Thank you."

He set her coffee cup into the sink. "Wouldn't want you to spill any coffee on this."

Mark removed both contracts as carefully as if they were delicate glass. They initialed each page, signed the backs and with a flourish he handed her a check large enough to keep Classy Creations in business for the next few months. Her pulse soared with elation, but she attempted to appear casual as she tucked the check into her purse.

Mark's gaze followed the baby sucking his ball. "You sure the baby can't choke on that?"

"Alex will be fine. The ball is way too large for him to get into his mouth." His odd comment was the last thing she'd expected. "I'll be in touch soon. My secretary is already sending out press releases for the announcements next week."

"I'm sure you'll do a good job. You came highly recommended."

Before she could decide whether to ask who had recommended her, because maybe she should remember, Jeff struggled through the garage door with a four-by-eight sheet of plywood.

Mark locked his briefcase and set it aside. "Here, let me help you with that."

Within minutes the two men had the window secured, darkening the room. An eerie tingle danced over Chelsea's spine, and as if sensing her mood, Alex fussed. She picked him up out of his swing and took comfort in his warm, wiggly little body.

After she thanked Mark for his help, he left. She still hadn't decided whether to accept Jeff's offer. She didn't want to depend upon him, didn't want him to help her out of pity and the innate compassion that was so much a part of him.

Jeff joined her and Alex in the den. The shifting sapphire lights in his eyes pierced her with unnamed longing. "I'll worry if I take you to a hotel. If you won't consider your safety, then stay with me for my state of mind. I'll sleep better if you're with me and I know you're safe."

And she'd sleep better knowing he was there. She turned to him with her hands on her hips, thinking it was unfair to let him get involved with her when she knew so little about her past. But memories of a bullet slamming into the wall convinced her. Alex's safety

was at stake. The baby had to come first. "Thank you.
But we may only stay one night."

His eyes mellowed with pleasure. "You can always
move to a hotel later if you feel the least bit uncomfortable at my place."

After making the decision, they loaded both cars in
the driveway with baby toys and paraphernalia and a
suitcase for Chelsea. Without regret, she left her house
with its boarded window behind.

In the driveway, Chelsea started her car to follow
Jeff into the street. Alex was strapped in his car seat,
holding his favorite stuffed monkey. Chelsea had almost turned into the street when a gray-haired woman
in an old Lincoln screeched to a halt in front of Chelsea's car to block her exit.

With a face mottled red with rage, the woman
rushed over and pounded the windshield of Chelsea's
car with her fist, screaming an invective.

# Chapter Eight

"Don't drive away!" the stranger screamed, her high-pitched tone more desperate than angry. "Please, I've got to talk to you."

The woman looked straight at Chelsea, and tears rained down her cheeks, mascara drizzled over her immaculately made-up face. She looked to be in her midfifties and was dressed in a double-breasted blazer that matched a button-front dress.

When Chelsea didn't drive off, the woman ceased pummeling the hood, dug into her purse for a tissue and dabbed at her anguished face. Cutting the car's engine, Chelsea cracked the window, her heart sputtering. "Can I help you?"

"I've been trying to reach you for weeks." She dabbed at her eyes, smearing the mascara even worse. Finally she gave up and crushed the tissue between her fingers. "Sandy said she asked you to talk to me—"

"Sandy?"

"—but when she told me that you were too busy, I didn't know what to believe. I thought I would have to take desperate action—"

Out of the corner of her eye, Chelsea saw Jeff put his car in reverse, park and join them. Since the woman now appeared harmless, Chelsea opened her door and stepped outside, anxious to clear up the stranger's identity. "Pounding on my window is desperate enough, don't you think?"

Her face pinkened in a sheepish expression. "I'm sorry. When you pulled out with all those boxes—" she gestured to the car "—I was afraid you were moving and I might not be able to find you again."

Chelsea kept hoping the woman would say something to indicate why she'd practically risked her life to stop her car, because Chelsea was just as baffled now as before.

"Do I know you?" she ventured, hoping the already on-the-edge-of-hysterical woman wouldn't turn out to be her mother.

"We met at an office party a year or two back. I'm Leslie Tinsdale, Martin Tinsdale's wife."

From the elegant way Leslie Tinsdale dressed, Chelsea would guess the woman didn't lose control like this often. Of course, fashion sense had nothing to do with emotional stability, but Mrs. Tinsdale's every hair was in place, her nails immaculately groomed, though her fingers clutched an old purse to her side as if ashamed of the worn leather. Come to think of it, while her clothes might once have been expensive, the style was dated.

"How can I help you, Mrs. Tinsdale?"

"Martin would kill me if he knew I was here."

Kill? The sun passed behind a cloud, leaving them standing in shadow, and a chill shivered down Chelsea's spine. If Leslie Tinsdale had come to warn her that Martin was the murderer, the police could arrest him, and Chelsea wouldn't have to leave her home and go into hiding.

Was Chelsea overreacting? From the suspicious look in Jeff's eyes, his thoughts were clearly moving along similar lines. Martin Tinsdale could be the man who had attacked her in the hospital, the one who had threatened her on the phone. The caller had said he, or she, was coming to collect what was owed. After working for over two decades, Martin Tinsdale might think Classy Creations should have been his. From what she'd learned, her former employee certainly had motive for revenge.

Before she jumped to conclusions, Chelsea needed more information. ''I see no reason to mention this conversation to your husband.'' She wouldn't even know Martin Tinsdale if she bumped right into him. ''We'll keep this between us.''

''I'm not here for a handout.''

Jeff came up beside her, ducked to check Alex, who was sleeping in his car seat, and placed a steadying hand on Chelsea's arm.

''Why *are* you here, Mrs. Tinsdale?'' Chelsea asked, feeling puzzled and wary but more sure of herself with Jeff by her side.

''Didn't Sandy tell you?''

Maybe Sandy had, and she'd forgotten. And then again, maybe she hadn't. Either way, Chelsea was impatient to resolve the mystery. ''Go on, please, Mrs. Tinsdale.''

The woman lifted her head and looked Chelsea straight in the eye. ''I'd like you to hire Martin back.'' She held up her hand as if to stop Chelsea's expected protest. ''I know you've been having cash-flow problems. Martin did business with the smaller retail establishments for years. He'd be vital to wooing them back.''

Welcome her enemy into the corporate fold where he'd have a better opportunity to track her and kill her? It should be out of the question, but Mrs. Tinsdale might be right. Classy Creations needed those accounts. And yet, although Chelsea couldn't recall her prior reasoning, she *had* fired the man. She couldn't forget he just might be the person who had shot out her window last night. Then again, she had not one shred of proof.

Still, condemning the man without meeting him didn't seem fair. That's why she'd already told Sandy to arrange a meeting next week. Apparently Mrs. Tinsdale had taken events into her own hands instead of waiting for Sandy's call. Recalling her secretary's insistence, Chelsea wondered what she still didn't know and sighed.

Meeting Martin on her own territory would probably be safe enough. After all, it was unlikely he'd attack her if he thought she was about to give him a job.

"I've already asked Sandy to arrange a meeting with your husband."

Mrs. Tinsdale's eyes brightened, then brimmed with tears and overflowed. Her voice choked up. "Thank you. You have no idea how much this opportunity will mean to Martin. He's a proud man. Being out of work has not been good for him."

"In what way, ma'am?" Jeff asked.

"A man thinks of himself by what he does—at least the men of my generation do. Like anyone, my husband needs to be useful."

After Mrs. Tinsdale started her car and drove away, Jeff shook his head with a sigh. "I'm not sure talking to her husband is a good idea. Do you think Martin Tinsdale could have—?"

She tried to stifle the fear that had never completely disappeared since the first attempt on her life. "That's why I want to meet him. He could be harboring a deep resentment against me." She sighed. "My employees don't seem to like me very much. The copy editor, Vanessa, won't look me in the eye. My accountant, Walter, is so sad I suspect he's hiding something. And Sandy, well, she pushed hard for me to talk to Martin Tinsdale. I wonder what her stake in this is?"

Jeff curled his arm over her shoulder and gave her a sideways hug. "I don't want you to take any risks."

She heard the caring in his tone and wondered if he was merely concerned for her safety or whether he would miss her if she was killed. Or both. She knew she'd regret dying without ever having made love to him. With firm resolve, she pushed the thought aside. Any deeper feelings between them had to remain on hold until her memory returned or until the police found Anne's killer.

Chelsea glanced at Alex. "I have more than myself to worry about now. I'll be careful."

She had to be careful for the sake of the baby sleeping in the car. He looked so innocent and peaceful. Poor tyke. She'd been his mother less than a week and they'd been chased in a taxi and had the front window of their house shot out of the frame. What kind of mess had she gotten him into? And now she had another worry. If the Carpenters found out about her problems, would a judge send the baby away?

DAMN HER! Chelsea Connors had no right keeping what did not belong to her. And she had the luck of the devil latching on to that doctor to save her miserable life.

Dr. Jeffrey Kendall's interference had begun to be tiresome. He must have said something to stop Chelsea's forward momentum. Outlined in her window, she'd presented a prime target. And a steady finger had pulled the trigger.

Only stopping short had prevented her from dying. But the doctor and confounded luck couldn't protect her forever.

Deft hands guided the iron over the newspaper, eliminating the creases in a soothing motion. Failure could not be tolerated. The repetitive motion of ironing gave the mind time to come up with an alternate plan.

She would run just like her friend had tried to run. And just like Anne, Chelsea would be tracked down and murdered. Or perhaps a faked suicide. Ah, yes. Perfect. The amnesia would cause her depression. Such poetic justice for the new mother, overwhelmed and despondent, to die by her own hand, her own gun.

The newspaper, crisp and warm, could wait until later to be read. It was time to make final preparations to leave town.

"SO HOW DID YOUR MEETING with Martin Tinsdale go?" Jeff asked.

During the ride Friday night to Benedict Academy's anniversary party seemed like the first moment Jeff had had Chelsea to himself all week. While she'd stayed at his home, she wrapped herself in her work and her child. She might be living under his roof, but ever since he'd hinted there could be no permanence to their relationship, she'd withdrawn as if preparing herself for a final goodbye.

The thought of losing her disturbed him more than he'd thought possible. Not for the first time, he found the prospect of spending his life without a wife or children lonely. He hadn't seen his own dad often. In eighteen years, his father never once came to his birthday party. He'd graduated first in his class, and Dad missed his high-school graduation to do a heart transplant. And when the patient, a four-year-old girl, died on the operating table, he'd been too down to celebrate his son's achievements. Jeff had been loved, but his day-to-day accomplishments couldn't compete with the crises of saving a life. He forgave his dad repeatedly. But it was no way for a child to grow up.

He would do everything in his power to keep another child from that kind of hurt, and Chelsea from the pain his mother had suffered over the years.

While they were together, he would do his best to keep her happy, protect her. But there were limits to what he could give to her. To any woman.

Live in the moment, he told himself. That's all he could have. And he hoped she'd enjoyed some of their time together, as well.

As he glanced at Chelsea, her lips parted, her eyes green, her skin gently flushed, he couldn't have said why he found her so endearing and charming. But she called to him on some elemental level that for the first time made him question his choice of career. For Jeff knew all too well that the schedules of a practicing cardiac surgeon and a father didn't mix well.

She tilted her head against the car window, either unconcerned about loosening the fancy twist of her hair before the party or so deep in thought she was oblivious to her actions. "I thought once I'd met Martin Tinsdale, I'd have a clearer picture of the situation. But now I'm more confused than ever."

He drove up the entrance ramp onto the freeway and tried to draw Chelsea out, preferring to think of anything but how much he wanted to take her in his arms and kiss her worries away. During the past week, his feelings had grown so strong he feared if he kissed her, he'd lose all control. So he welcomed the distraction of a discussion. "Did you sense a threat?"

"Martin is a gentleman, polished, polite, proud. Although he tried to hide his resentment, once or twice during our conversation, I caught a glimpse of outrage in his eyes before he turned away."

His fist clenched at the thought of someone hurting her. "You think he could turn violent?"

"I don't know. He might simply be frustrated that he no longer has a career in the firm he worked twenty years to build." She ran a hand through her bangs and chewed her lower lip. "In a way, he was right. If Classy Creations still had those smaller accounts, we wouldn't be in dire financial circumstances."

One of the traits Jeff admired most about Chelsea was her ability to look at a problem from different angles. But he wasn't so sure he liked the thought of her having direct contact with Tinsdale on a daily basis. He tried to keep his possessive protectiveness from his tone. "Are you going to hire him back?"

Jeff's gaze flickered from the road to the rearview mirror and the baby strapped into the passenger seat, then to Chelsea's face and back to the road. Her shuttered look left him with the impression that she'd made a decision but didn't want to tell him because she knew he wouldn't approve.

"Martin Tinsdale is fifty-five years old. At his age, it's difficult to find a job."

His stomach flip-flopped. "You rehired him, didn't you?"

"Even if he's after me, he doesn't need to work at my office to find me."

"He may have tried to shoot you."

"It's just a hunch, but I don't think so. I have a feeling Martin is too proud to resort to violence."

Jeff refrained from pointing out that she could be staking her life on a hunch. Besides, after he ruthlessly shelved his concern for her safety, he realized she did have a point. If Martin Tinsdale wanted her dead, he needn't work at Classy Creations to kill her. As Jeff joined the line of cars pulling up to the gate that led to Benedict Academy, Chelsea dug her invitation out of her purse. "I hope Ms. Kilcuddy is on time. Mark said there's a back room where she can watch Alex."

Jeff showed their invitation to the uniformed guard posted at the wrought-iron gate. The cadet waved them inside with a spotless white glove. "Good of her to watch Alex."

The immaculate grounds with stone fences separating orchards and fields reminded Jeff of a parklike setting. Wide running paths and various exercise stations constructed of natural materials complemented the natural beauty and no doubt enhanced the rigorous training necessary to become an officer in the United States military.

Large oaks canopied the paved road. Sunlight peeked through, and the last blossoms of summer heralded the coming autumn.

And just as the seasons inevitably changed, so did progress. Many generals and politicians had been educated at Benedict Academy, a school that only accepted the crème de la crème of high-school graduates. Chelsea's top-notch selling job aside, the place was steeped in tradition. The old guard might not welcome her radical plan.

While her idea to encourage woman to enroll in the school would be praised by some alumni, Jeff suspected the majority would be stunned by tonight's announcement. Having the press there for the festivities would help calm the backlash, for no politician wanted to insult a large number of voters. And even if there were complaints, they wouldn't be loud or vocal—not with the liberal press sure to take up Chelsea's promotion with enthusiasm.

Strange how his thoughts ran to protecting Chelsea. He'd called the police during the week to find out if they had any leads concerning who might be after her. The detective admitted only that most of her employees had alibis the night of the shooting. Only Sandy, the secretary, Vanessa, the copy editor, and Walter, the accountant, had been off alone. But just because they couldn't prove their innocence didn't make them guilty. Tom and Mary Carpenter vouched for one another's whereabouts, each claiming the other was watching television at home. And Martin Tinsdale had been out walking his dog. However, he lived a convenient ten-minute drive from Chelsea's house.

A waltz played by the school's famed band broke into his thoughts. The strains wafted through the air as one of the cadets gave them a voucher and parked their car. Jeff helped Chelsea by carrying the stroller up the steps into the brick gymnasium.

Carpets had been rolled out along the gymnasium floor, and tables set with orchid-and-miniature-ivy centerpieces surrounded the elaborate buffet of gleaming silver dishes on the finest lace cloth. Crystal flutes stood waiting to be filled by uniformed cadets. Bottles of champagne cooled in sterling ice buckets. For those who preferred hard liquor, an open bar stood discreetly under the raised basketball backboard. Toward the front of the gym, where the band played, a dais with a lectern and microphones waited for the speeches to come.

They were early, and the room remained relatively empty, although some guests had started to arrive. Chelsea waved to one of her employees, but headed toward a side room off to the left marked Coach. "Mark said Alex should be fine in here."

"You don't think you're overdoing the protective-mother bit?" Jeff teased, wondering if she could hear the admiration in his tone.

"I didn't want to leave Alex at home."

"You just don't look motherly in that dress," he added, enjoying the blush that rose to her cheeks. She looked fantastic. Her eyes sparkled, and it took all his control not to kiss her senseless. Every man in the room would be staring at her, and he'd have to be careful not to deck one of them. As much as he was beginning to wish otherwise, he reminded himself Chelsea was not his.

Wearing a sequined spaghetti-strapped black dress and matching jacket that hugged her curves and seemed to change colors as she walked, she looked drop-dead gorgeous. Her hair, arranged in an elegant French twist, revealed the fine lines of her neck and emphasized her high cheekbones. He'd been anticipating this night all week long, eager to see Chelsea decked out in her finest clothes to savor her business triumph. But it was her shimmering eyes dancing with excitement that made accompanying her a pleasure.

Jeff held open the door to the coach's office. Chelsea rolled Alex into the room and greeted the woman from foster care. "Hi. Thanks for agreeing to watch Alex on such short notice."

Ms. Kilcuddy's booming voice greeted them with enthusiasm. "I'm glad for the extra time with the little one." From behind her glasses, she took in the three of them. "And aren't you all looking mighty fine. Chelsea, dear, I wouldn't haven't recognized you and the handsome doctor. You're a far sight prettier without that bandage on your head."

"Jeff removed my stitches today." She pushed Alex's stroller into the cozy office, bent and retrieved a bag stowed behind the baby's seat. "Here's formula and diapers, a change of clothes, toys and a blanket."

"Now don't you worry none, dear. I've been watching little darlings all my life. I like Alex and he likes me." Ms. Kilcuddy shooed her on her way. "You go on and have a good time."

Vanessa, the red-haired copy editor, stuck her head around the door. "Ms. Connors?"

"Coming," Chelsea replied.

Jeff placed his hand lightly on the small of her back, a gesture he'd been anticipating since he'd first seen her in that dress. Of course, touching her back wasn't all he wanted to do. Her upswept hair left him a clear path to her neck, and he imagined planting a slew of tiny kisses from her collarbone to her earlobe.

Only one part of her outfit jarred him—the tiny black-and-gold ornaments dangling from her ears.

There was nothing wrong with her earrings. He'd just have preferred seeing her in his grandmother's diamonds. The sparkling heirlooms would have matched the glimmer in her eyes, but the earrings represented more than jewelry to Jeff. Even lending her the diamonds would have marked her as his—a commitment he'd vowed not to make. Yet for all his determination to leave the earrings in the vault, every time he glanced at Chelsea, he imagined them on her ears.

"Mr. Lindstrom wanted you to know they're almost ready for the introductions," Vanessa chattered without once looking her in the eye. "Mick is fussing that someone bent the corner of his art, but I think he's just showing off for that graphic-designer friend of his. And Walter is looking so sad—he didn't bring a date. I think some woman stood him up."

Jeff looked over Vanessa's head at Chelsea. "I think I'll get a drink. Want anything?"

"A club soda. Thanks. I've a feeling I'll need a clear head tonight."

"I've seen you in action. You'll be fine."

Jeff winked and Chelsea caught her breath as desire struck her core. He looked so handsome in a suit and tie, the dark navy serge highlighting those intelligent eyes. All week he'd kept his word. There had been no shared kisses, no caresses, not even a hug. Just as he'd promised, he given her a roof over her head and more than enough room to think about him.

And she was just as confused now as the first time he'd hinted that a commitment between them was impossible. She'd tried to keep busy with work and Alex. She should be exhausted. Instead, she felt wound up tighter than a top set to spin into orbit.

The tension simmering all week had suddenly reached the boiling point. Tonight sizzling attraction had erupted, making her aware of Jeff's every admiring glance, the huskiness in his tone, the jaunty I'll-catch-up-with-you-later gleam she saw in his eyes before he walked away from her.

Pushing thoughts of Jeff aside with difficulty, she hurried for a last-minute word with her employees. Vanessa slipped into the crowd. The room had quickly filled with guests, but Chelsea easily spied Mick in his yellow velveteen tux. The art director was smoothing out a bent corner of the art, and she expected him to fuss.

Instead, Mick discreetly led her aside, his limp still distinct, and whispered in her ear, "The press is buzzing. They sense something's up. I'd suggest making the announcement as soon as possible before they pry it out of one of us."

Chelsea nodded. "Thanks, Mick. Have you seen Sandy?"

Her art director frowned. "She was looking for you."

"Not to worry, I'll find her."

Mark Lindstrom emerged from the crowd, handsome in his spotless gray dress uniform decorated with multicolored ribbons. "There are a few people I'd like you to meet."

While the reporters milled at the entrance, waiting to snap questions at the arriving military brass, Mark introduced her to members of Benedict Academy's board of directors. Chelsea smiled and reassured the gentlemen they would be happy with their decision to admit women after they saw the school's increased enrollment. She praised them for their modern ideas, all the while keeping her eye out for her employees.

She saw Walter Brund by himself, leaning morosely against a wall and downing what looked like straight Scotch. Vanessa was flirting with a general old enough to be her grandfather, but the redhead's gaze followed Mark Lindstrom as if she had a crush on their client. And Mick was guarding the storyboards with sheer coquetry, daring anyone to remove the sheet covering the art before her presentation.

But where was Sandy?

Jeff returned with her club soda and whisked her away to escort her toward the dais where Mark Lindstrom would introduce her. A cadet tapped the microphone and asked the milling crowd to take their seats.

Chelsea spotted Sandy, who was signaling her with a frantic expression on her face, but it was too late for Chelsea to go to her. Knowing Sandy's message would have to wait, Chelsea swallowed her unease.

Mark had removed his glasses, cleaned them with a folded square of tissue, then replaced them on the bridge of his nose. He introduced Classy Creations, and Chelsea sipped her club soda nervously. Her speech would be followed by one from the school's most famous alumnus, a Gulf War hero who'd used his military career as a stepping stone to a seat in the Senate.

Jeff squeezed her hand for luck, then left her sitting in the glaring lights, a perfect target. *Don't even think it.* With all the military personnel surrounding her, no one would dare draw a gun here.

She missed Mark Lindstrom's opening words, but when he held out his arm to her and the audience applauded, Chelsea rose to her feet in nervous expectation. As she started her speech, the lights dimmed. A movie screen descended from the ceiling, and slides depicted the campaign in vivid color while she narrated.

Speaking quickly and concisely, she laid out the future of Benedict Academy and the concept of welcoming women to enroll in the prestigious institution. She paused once to take a sip from her glass and thought she heard Alex cry. But her faith in Ms. Kilcuddy prevented her from worrying.

She finished to a round of applause, deftly responded to a few questions from the press, then returned the microphone to Mark Lindstrom. The room buzzed with the news, and she sensed reporters itching to leave and file their stories, though they stayed in order to hear the senator's speech. Chelsea listened politely, but was glad when she could finally stand and move about.

Mark came over and shook her hand. "You did a great job. Nice presentation."

Within moments a crowd surrounded them, and minutes passed before she could break free. She wanted to talk to Jeff. And she needed to check on Alex.

Walter loomed out of the crowd, her first employee to offer his compliments. "I just want to congratulate you. Anne would have been proud."

About to say a quick thanks and turn away, Chelsea fastened her attention on her accountant. "Anne?"

Walter's drink sloshed over his hand. "I still miss her, don't you?"

He didn't act as if he expected an answer, but rather as if his question was hypothetical. But replying seemed the safest way to go unless she wanted to admit to her missing memories. "She was my best friend."

"Mine, too. Did she tell you she'd accepted my proposal before...?"

Proposal? Walter and Anne had been dating? Damn it, her lack of memory had never been so inconvenient. Luckily Walter was too drunk to notice Chelsea's astonishment.

He rambled on. "If only my mother hadn't insisted I visit her that day, I would have been there to protect Anne. I loved her so much. Why did she have to leave me?"

So Walter wasn't a suspect in Anne's murder, not if he had an alibi. But then what mother wouldn't lie to save her son? "Anne didn't leave you. She was murdered. And she must have loved you very much to agree to marry you."

"I told her I wanted Alex." Walter staggered, then caught his balance with a look of apology. "You'll do fine by him. Wouldn't be right for a single man to raise him alone."

Oh, no! Had she found Anne's lover and Alex's father? Chelsea's knees almost buckled, and she steadied herself by putting a hand to the wall. The swirling crowd of people left them in a pocket of privacy. Unwilling to draw attention to herself, Chelsea fought to keep her tone normal.

"Walter, is Alex your son?"

"Almost."

Chelsea wanted to scream. Instead, she lowered her tone. "Almost? What does that mean? Either Alex is your son or he isn't."

At that moment Sandy dashed up, almost bumping into Chelsea. "Alex was crying earlier. I couldn't find you, and then you had to make your speech."

She turned to Sandy with a worried frown. "Is Alex all right?"

"That's the problem. He and Ms. Kilcuddy are gone!"

Terror froze Chelsea to the spot. She couldn't have heard right. "What?"

"Well, all Alex's stuff is in the coach's office, but I can't find your baby-sitter or Alex, either."

Jeff joined her, apparently overhearing the last of Sandy's words. "Don't panic, maybe Ms. Kilcuddy just took him for a walk."

Chelsea clutched Jeff's hand like a drowning woman about to plunge over Niagara Falls. Her limbs suddenly twitched into action. "Let's see if they're back."

Jeff shouldered his way through the crowd, tugging her through behind him. It seemed like a year before they reached the coach's office to find Ms. Kilcuddy barging out through the door, a frown of concern on her face. "Really dear, I just slipped off to the rest room after Alex fell asleep. There was no need for you to disturb him."

"I don't have Alex."

Behind her bottle-lens glasses, Ms. Kilcuddy's eyes widened and her face paled. "But...but...Alex isn't old enough to crawl out of his stroller."

Jeff squeezed Chelsea's hand and then let go. "Stay here. I'll tell Mark to make an announcement and ask whoever has Alex to bring him back to the coach's office.''

Vanessa joined the little group, took one look at Chelsea and asked, ''What's wrong?''

''Alex is gone. Have you seen him?''

Vanessa's face turned so ashen her freckles stood out like oil stains on a white beach. ''No. This can't be happening.''

As much as Chelsea wanted to shake the girl, she refrained. ''Did you see anyone come in here? Do you have any idea where Alex could be?''

Vanessa's hands rose to her temples. ''Give me a moment to think.''

# Chapter Nine

"What's there to think about? Either you've seen Alex or you haven't," Chelsea nearly screamed, her heart pounding her ribs.

"I try not to look at the baby," Vanessa said. She swallowed. "I... he reminds me of the son I gave up for adoption."

"You saw someone leave this room?" Chelsea asked, ignoring the girl's grim tone.

Vanessa nodded. "I was looking down. But whoever he was wore boots and a uniform."

Chelsea hurried to the door and flung it open. At least a hundred uniformed men stood talking, eating and strolling around the buffet tables. She spied Jeff speaking to a cadet who pointed across the room.

Her gaze followed his motion, and she spied Mark Lindstrom. And Alex!

She, Jeff, Vanessa and Sandy reached Mark at about the same time. Vanessa glanced at Mark as if he was a hero but scowled when Sandy placed her hand on Mark's forearm. A muscle in Jeff's jaw pulsed as he contained his anger for Mark's causing such worry.

Mark faced them all with a disapproving shake of his head. "There you are. I've been looking for you."

Mark handed her the baby, and she quickly checked him over. Alex seemed fine. But from the past few minutes of worry, she must have lost a year off her life. "How did . . . ? Why did—?"

"I stopped by to tell you that you wowed the board." Mark mopped baby drool off his uniform with barely concealed distaste. "Anyway, you weren't around. Alex was crying and the sitter was nowhere in sight. So I picked him up and have been searching for you ever since."

PLEASANTLY EXHAUSTED but too tired to sleep, Chelsea had returned to Jeff's house happy with the way the evening had gone, yet at the same time numbed by the responsibility of watching Alex. She'd almost panicked at the simple misunderstanding, and the thought of losing him scared her frantic.

After changing into jeans and sweater, Chelsea sat curled in the center of Jeff's futon, ensconced on the back porch amid ten acres of lush estate along Chesapeake Bay. "I don't know if I'm ready for this."

"Ready for what?"

"Parenthood." She stared out over the sparkling water, glinting like jewels on black velvet beneath the moonlight, tucked her bare feet under her, drew her arms around her knees.

Jeff slid beside her and draped his arm around her shoulders. "Every parent momentarily loses a child at one time or another. You'll be holding a hand in a grocery store, let go to reach for some soup and look down to find the child has wandered off. It happens."

"I almost lost it."

"You're new at this parenting business. Give yourself a chance."

"But can I count on myself to do what's best for Alex?"

"Why the doubts? Because you're lacking memories or experience?" He massaged her shoulders, his fingers loosening the knots. "Are you afraid to believe in yourself?"

"I just wish my memories would return. Alex is a big responsibility. At the party when the baby disappeared, I even suspected Ms. Kilcuddy of wrongdoing." Her head slumped back against his arm. "How do I know whom I can trust?"

He gently cupped her chin and turned her head toward him. "Believe in yourself," he whispered, seemingly mesmerized by what he saw in her eyes. "I do."

She raised her mouth, wound her arms around his neck and kissed him. Desire fierce enough to splinter her heart frightened her. She reminded herself Dr. Jeffrey Kendall, soon-to-be cardiac surgeon, didn't have time in his life for a wife and child. There could be nothing permanent between them. But she didn't let go.

Even knowing there would be no easy goodbyes, that the eventual break would be intense, sorrowful and haunting, she wanted him enough at this moment to risk the consequences later. They'd already shared too much for there ever to be a clean parting between them. And she wanted him too badly not to use every feminine weapon she had to change his mind. Gambling that the chemistry between them might sway his final decision in her favor, she tossed caution aside.

"Make love to me."

"Chelsea?" His husky tone told her he wanted her to be sure of her decision.

"I'm sure."

"And what if you discover a long-lost boyfriend tomorrow?"

"Then I'll deal with him tomorrow." She shot him an impish grin. "The chance of that occurring is unlikely. Sandy told me I'm pretty much a loner, working most Friday and Saturday nights. In my personal planner, I couldn't find any notations that even hinted at the possibility of a date."

She reached out and touched his face. His cheek felt hard, smooth, and she caught just a hint of tensed muscles in his jaw. "So you see, you have me all to yourself."

The contact, the simple grazing of her fingertips against his chin, ignited a passion that incinerated the barriers between them. Eagerly she turned, pressed her chest to his until he lay flat on his back. He gazed at her with such hunger, by fierce look alone, he set her aflame.

"Tell me that making love is like riding a bicycle," she murmured.

"What?"

She chuckled. "Well, I know what's going to happen, but as for specifics...I can't remember."

He groaned. "Tell me you aren't a virgin."

She giggled and pulled her sweater over her head. "Do I look virginal?" she teased, knowing his gaze was drawn to her lacy bra.

He lifted his mouth to sear a path across her lips. "Are you trying to torture me, woman?"

"I hadn't planned on it." She sat up straight. "But now that you mention it, if I were going to torture you—" her fingers went to the clasp of her bra "—I'd do this."

The snap sounded loudly in the crisp night air. For a moment, the crickets ceased their song. A night bird cawed.

Her move felt bold, yet she was glad for the dimness of the half-moon that hid the momentary awkwardness running through her. Doubts assailed her.

"I love the way your skin reflects the silvery moonlight," he told her, and the husky catch in his tone banished the last of her qualms. "And you're soft so soft. Like gossamer."

He grazed the undersides of her breasts with a tantalizing caress of his thumbs, his gaze never wavering from her face. A brief shiver rippled through her, and she wriggled eagerly against him, pressing for more.

"Tell me what you like," he whispered.

"Cotton candy, the scent of baby powder—"

His fingers flicked her nipples, and she gasped as a streak of meteor fire shot through her.

In the moonlight, his eyes darkened, his lips turned up suggestively. "Tell me how you want me to make love to you."

He drew an answer from deep inside her, and only her confidence in him allowed her to voice her desire. "Love me slowly. As if neither of us has ever done this before."

Nervously she unbuttoned his shirt, and her fingers explored. His chest was warm, muscular, hot. His clean male scent mixed with the tangy air of the sea and the perfume of fresh-cut roses on a coffee table beside them.

"Your jeans," he murmured, his fingers unbuttoning, unzipping, then pushing the denim over her hips.

She removed his shirt, his slacks, and then they clung together on the futon, his lips kissing hers. The night air nipped at her skin, but her chills and goose bumps had nothing to do with the outdoor temperature and everything to do with the rush of excitement flowing through her.

His limbs intertwined with hers, and he rose above her, his hand reaching for a rose.

"Be careful of the thorns."

He twisted the stem between his fingers. "Ah, this hothouse variety has no thorns."

He raised the blossom to her nostrils, and she inhaled the sweet scent. When he traced the petal over her cheek, across the hollows of her collarbone, and swirled the blossom over her breasts, she was unprepared for the exquisite sensation that curled her toes. Or the way he stared at every flicker of her pleasure, learning the sensitive hollows of her stomach, the curves of her hips.

"That tickles."

"Does not," he insisted, dipping the flower lower.

"Does, too." With a mischievous grin, she snatched the stem from his hand. "Two can play this game, mister."

With an impatient sigh, he chuckled and clasped his hands behind his head. "Do with me what you will."

"Ah, I fully intend to." She swished the petals over his lips and under his nose. With a soft chuckle, she murmured, "It's time you smelled the roses, Doctor."

When she traced a path along the side of his neck to his nipples, he sucked in his breath. "I don't think I'll ever look at a rose in quite the same way again."

"And what about me? Will you still respect me in the morning?" she teased, and tugged off his boxer shorts, pleased he wanted her as much as she wanted him.

"More. I'll respect you more."

Glad that he found her femininity so arousing, she grew bolder. She skimmed the petals over the length of him, wondering how long his patience would last.

Still she jumped, startled, when moments later his hand snapped out and grasped her wrist. "You've had your way with me long enough, woman."

Afraid she would never have enough but unable to avoid the heat seeking to embroil her, she yielded to the heady sensations that raged like wildfire after a slow-building burn. He removed her panties, and then it was his turn to tease her with the flower. When she could no longer bear the sweet torture on her breasts and belly, she reached for him.

"Uh-uh." She heard husky laughter in his tone. "The lady requested slow lovemaking, and slow is what she'll get."

The flower delved between her legs, and she whimpered in delight and anticipation. Her hips twisted on the futon. Her parted thighs welcomed him.

When he rolled away, she wanted to yank him back. But he wasn't leaving her permanently, only reaching for his shirt to tug at the front pocket.

"Got it." With a triumphant grin, he held a foil packet between thumb and forefinger. He ripped the packet open and grinned. "I bought this yesterday— just for us."

She held out her palm, and he handed it to her. And she did a little impish exploring of her own.

Suddenly his body lay hard atop hers, and his hands cupped the sides of her face. As he slid into her, filling her, he stared into her eyes, their gazes locking and holding, heightening her awareness. For a moment, she thought she stared into his soul. She ached to prolong the intimacy and hold completely still, but she didn't have the power to resist the fires he'd kindled.

Scorching with need, she rocked her hips. His gaze still locked with hers. And infinitely slowly he pulled back, and somehow she knew the bliss on her face heightened his own. Her fingers gripped his shoulders, urging him faster, but he maintained the same exquisitely slow pace until their breaths came in gasps. Her heart pounded in her chest.

His fingers still cupped her face. Their locked gazes bonded them in a joining of body and soul. And as the aching sensation swelled to dazzling release and she yielded to the cresting wave of pleasure inside her, he took that in, too, making the ripples of bliss his own.

With her name on his lips, followed by a deep groan, he surrendered. Through the ebbing tide of her own pleasure, she raised her hips to meet his last, frantic thrusts. With a long, shuddering sigh, he spent himself deep within her. His body went still, but his fingers twined in her hair and pulled her closer.

She snuggled her head to his shoulder, pressed a kiss to his neck. Love surged through her, and she almost drowned in the sweet tenderness of the moment. Surely her feelings couldn't be one-sided.

But he didn't speak, just clasped her close to his thudding heart and left her to wonder if their lovemaking had carried him away on the same wondrous feeling.

EVER SINCE they'd made love last night, Chelsea had been unusually quiet. Jeff hadn't pressed her. Yet he wasn't such an insensitive clod that he couldn't guess what she wanted. Commitment.

Although he suspected making love had affected her as deeply as it had him, he was happy to keep their relationship the way it was. And she hadn't said one word. So why was he feeling so damned guilty?

They were adults. She'd come to him. She hadn't been drunk but had decided of her own free will. She'd known up front that he couldn't give her everything.

And yet even he knew relationships didn't remain still forever. He would have to decide how much she meant to him. But how could he measure his feelings when she kept his emotions in such a swirling state?

He'd hinted to her he couldn't give any more than he'd already given. But could he?

He squeezed the steering wheel hard. No other woman had ever made him question his plans the way Chelsea did. But then no one had ever made him feel the way she did—happy to be alive. From the first moment he'd seen her, before she'd opened her eyes, he'd sensed his attraction to her. And once he'd gotten to know her, she'd drawn him with a combination of pixie vulnerability and amazon inner strength. He'd tried to walk away—he should have run.

And yet he didn't regret one moment they'd spent together.

"Walter didn't sound pleased when I called." Chelsea shuffled the pages of her appointment book while Jeff drove toward her accountant's house.

Jeff caught the rattle Alex just dropped and handed it back to the baby, who was strapped into the seat behind them. "Well, it is Saturday, and you gave everyone the day off."

As the baby chewed on the rattle, Chelsea sighed. "I don't think Walter's problem has to do with wanting Saturday morning off."

"Why?"

She shrugged, unwilling to say more. "It's just a feeling." She drummed her fingers on the appointment book. "I met with him often until Anne's death. But in the last few weeks, we didn't have one meeting. Don't you think that odd?"

"Your meetings could have been about the firm's solvency and have had nothing to do with Anne."

"Maybe."

Jeff pulled into the driveway in a middle-class subdivision. Aside from the factor of protecting her, he was not quite sure why he'd insisted on accompanying her this morning. He was as anxious as Chelsea to discover whether Walter claimed to be the baby's father, but he didn't wish to examine or explore why he was so curious. He shoved the question firmly out of mind.

He parked, unstrapped Alex and lifted him to his shoulder. Stepping onto the driveway, he noted the house was in fine repair. From a few stray telltale blades of grass, Jeff guessed Walter must have just neatly trimmed the sidewalks. He was surprised to see a tricycle parked inside the open garage, and from the look on Chelsea's face when she saw it, she hadn't known Walter had children.

They walked along the concrete front walk, and Jeff admired the ruler-straight trimmed hedges, the eaves sparkling as if the house were recently pressure washed, the freshly painted front door.

Chelsea rang the bell, and Walter opened the door. She hadn't exaggerated his size; the man was built like a refrigerator and he towered over Jeff's six feet. How he'd missed Walter's hulking height at the party, he attributed to the large crowd.

Walter held out his hand for Jeff to shake, then stepped back. "Come in."

He led them to an immaculate living room, done in dark browns and deep-colored woods. "Can I get you something to drink?"

They declined and took seats on the couch. Walter slouched into a recliner, his palms marking a sweaty streak on the vinyl hand rests. "Tell me what I can do for you, Ms. Connors. Is the bank giving us problems again?"

She shook her head. "You told me at the party that you were almost Alex's father. What did you mean?"

The large man seemed to shrivel in the chair. His shoulders sagged, and his chin drooped until his neck almost disappeared. "After Anne said she'd marry me, I offered to adopt Alex."

Chelsea leaned forward, face tense. "What did Anne say?"

"Oh, she agreed. She thought I'd make a fine dad. We celebrated by buying a tricycle." He sighed. "I suppose I should give it to one of the neighborhood kids, but I just haven't gotten around to it."

Chelsea stiffened until she held her shoulders ramrod straight, and Jeff sensed her gearing up for the big question. "So when you said Alex was almost your son, you meant you were going to adopt him?"

"Yeah."

"Forgive me for asking such a personal question, but I have good reason to ask. Are you Alex's birth father?"

Walter frowned, and his brows knit over his nose. "You know that's impossible. I didn't meet Anne until after she was pregnant."

Clearly Chelsea didn't intend to tell Walter about her amnesia, but by the odd way Walter stared at her, he suspected something amiss. Jeff cleared his throat and asked the question Chelsea couldn't without revealing her memory loss. "How far along was Anne when you met her?"

"A month."

"Could she have lied to you?" Jeff asked.

Puppy-dog eyes reflected Walter's hurt. "Why would she do that?"

Jeff shifted the baby to his other shoulder. "Do you know who Alex's birth father is?"

"I never asked. Talking about the baby's father brought up bad memories for her. After the rough time she went through, I wanted her to have peace."

Some people thought of death as peaceful, but Jeff couldn't detect a violent bone in Walter's large body. He just couldn't picture the accountant resorting to shooting Chelsea to get back his son. Besides, if he were the real father, he could go to court and easily fight for parental privilege.

Jeff was ready to leave when Chelsea spoke up. "She never told me much about the father."

Walter looked a bit startled. "You and Carol were her best friends."

"Carol?"

Walter frowned. "I assumed you knew her. Carol Oxford runs the Oxford Inn in Old Point Comfort. Anne stayed there with Carol until you helped her move and find a new job. I thought she confided in you."

"Anne was a private person."

Walter covered his face with his large palms.

Jeff saw the big man's shoulders heave and spoke to him softly. "Thanks for talking to us. We'll see ourselves out."


"WALTER COULD HAVE LIED to us." That evening over dinner, while Jeff's sister Stacy baby-sat Alex, Chelsea sipped a glass of white wine, her fingers drumming the linen tablecloth. She'd tried to call Carol Oxford at the inn, but had been informed by a receptionist that the woman was out of town until tomorrow evening.

As Jeff played with his wineglass, she recalled those same hands teasing her, exciting her, pleasing her, and knew she couldn't make love to him again. Going home tomorrow would be difficult enough without stronger ties to bind her heart.

While she didn't regret making love, apparently she didn't mean as much to Jeff as she'd hoped. Unwilling to settle for half measures, she knew it was time to leave. A tightness in her chest refused to ease. She'd gambled and lost. And once she left him, she'd pay for it with loneliness, might-have-beens and second thoughts of what she could have done to make things turn out differently.

Swallowing the achy lump in her throat, she stared across the table at Jeff, memorizing a picture that would last when he was no longer around. His cropped hair surrounded a face filled with concern. And his eyes radiated compassion. More than any other characteristic, his eyes drew her. And his husky voice, so deeply modulated, tempted her to stay, evoking the comforting image of curling into the warmth of an afghan.

Not only must she leave for her own sake, but for Alex's sake, as well, before he grew attached to Jeff. The word *father* reminded her of the problem at hand. The mystery of Alex's birth father haunted her.

"You still think Walter is Alex's father?" she asked Jeff.

"I don't know."

She fiddled with her dinnerware. "According to Walter, we know Anne moved and changed jobs shortly after she became pregnant. He made it sound almost as if she was trying to get away from Alex's father."

With a tantalizing turn of his lips, he raised one dark brow. "But?"

"Suppose Anne moved because she found a new job—and then she met Walter. Perhaps Anne talked me into hiring him."

"You're guessing."

"True. But Walter was fired from his previous job, and the timing fits. From his file, I can't figure out why else I would have hired him."

"Is he competent?"

"I think so."

"Maybe that soft heart of yours wanted to give him a second chance."

Why did Jeff insist she had a soft heart when everything she'd learned about herself led her to think she'd been a cold businesswoman with few friends or hobbies outside of work? Clearly Jeff saw her differently than she saw herself.

"I do seem to have surrounded my self with people who aren't particularly fond of me. And then there are the Carpenters."

"They haven't backed off?"

"They're proceeding through the courts to win custody, but unless they find another will, my attorney doesn't think I should worry."

"I don't want you to worry, either. How's Martin Tinsdale working out?" Jeff broke off a piece of bread and buttered it in swift, sure strokes. She had to push her thoughts away from recalling the way his hands stroked her. Blast. Why did his every movement remind her of making love?

She forced herself to recall his question. "Martin's a wonder. He's already brought back four accounts. My employees like him. Sandy keeps telling me I did the right thing by rehiring him."

"And what do you think?"

"He's making my life easier. He's just as capable of running the firm as I am."

"But if he were angry, can you picture him taking a potshot at you?"

She hated suspecting every person she knew. She was tired of not remembering. She was tired of analyzing her every move. And she realized she couldn't spend another day, week or month waiting for Jeff to tell her what she wanted to hear.

She had to accept that Jeff simply wasn't the kind of man who could commit to marriage.

Reaching across the table, she took his hand, allowing herself the pleasure of touching him—just one more memory to pack away with the others. "I'm moving back home tomorrow."

Alarm brightened his eyes. "It's not safe."

"It may never be safe," she countered, swallowing the lump in her throat.

His hand tightened on hers. "If that's what you want. But you know you're welcome to stay."

She ignored the wrench of her heart. "I'm not the kind of woman to play house. And even if I were, Alex needs..."

"A father." Jeff's eyes filled with pain before he hid his anguish behind a shuttered look.

The rest of dinner passed in long silences. Chelsea barely tasted her food. She didn't finish her wine. Jeff paid their bill and without conferring, they skipped the movie they'd planned to see and drove back to Jeff's house.

Chelsea wanted to slide into the middle of the front seat, snuggle up to Jeff and rest her head on his shoulder. He always smelled so good. And his arm would curl around her in a comforting gesture. Only she didn't want comfort; she wanted love.

Why did she have to find the perfect man—kind, compassionate, sexy—and then discover he couldn't give her the one thing she wanted most? Life wasn't fair, and if she knew what religion she was, she might be tempted to raise her fist and shake it at God.

Instead, she grabbed hold of the thought that she wouldn't go home to an empty house. She would have Alex. She must make the right decision for her son.

"I've never thanked you for all your help," she said quietly, keeping tears at bay.

"Don't."

She heard the pain in his voice but she didn't care. If she meant so much to him, he could damned well do something about it.

"I'm not asking you to give up your profession."
She clamped her hand over her mouth. She wouldn't
resort to begging. She'd promised herself she would
leave with dignity, wouldn't say a word to castigate his
decision.

"I know. But it's not fair for you to live with a husband who is gone most of the time."

She sighed. "And who appointed you the one to
make this decision?"

He started to reply, but she raised her hand to his
lips. "Shh. We've been over this before. Let's not ruin
what we had together with words we may regret."

The cellular phone in his car rang and interrupted
their conversation. Jeff pushed a button.

The frantic voice of his sister Stacy shouted over the
speaker. "Jeff, someone's broken into the house!"

He stomped on the gas, and the car shot forward.
"Stacy, grab the baby and get out."

"I called 911," she cried. "They told me not to
hang up, but I did to call you."

Chelsea's heart pumped harder than the car's
screaming engine. "Where's Alex?"

"Upstairs. And I hear thumping noises. I c-can't
leave him. But I'm so scared."

Jeff whirled around a corner, tires squealing though
his voice remained calm. "It's going to be okay."

"I don't know what to do," Stacy cried. "Tell me
what to do."

"Leave the house," Chelsea ordered, hoping she
was making the right decision, fear and adrenaline
roaring through her like a hurricane.

Stacy sobbed. "But Alex?"

Jeff's sister was fifteen years old, five foot three and
a hundred pounds—no match for a dangerous and

possibly armed adult. But nausea roiled in Chelsea's stomach at the thought of Alex alone in his crib. Still, for Stacy to try to save the baby would put both of them at risk. Swallowing her fear and knowing that at the breakneck speed Jeff was driving, they'd arrive in minutes, Chelsea shouted in the direction of the phone. "A burglar will have no interest in a baby. Get out of there. Now!"

"Oh, noooo. The noises are directly over my head. Hurry, Jeff."

And then the line went dead.

# Chapter Ten

Sweat broke out on Chelsea's forehead and trickled into her eyes. *He'll be fine. He'll be okay.* She repeated the words like a mantra.

They were almost there. For once she wished Jeff lived in a subdivision. Even if Stacy ran for help, the neighboring estate was a good sprint through the surrounding woods. And in the meantime, Alex was vulnerable.

Jeff peeled around another corner, and she started to take off her seat belt. Jeff shook his head. "It could be dangerous. Wait in the car."

"That's my son in your house."

"I'll bring him to you."

She didn't waste breath arguing. Jeff turned into the winding driveway, and dust billowed behind them like a storm cloud. After he screeched to a stop, she leapt out of the car, held her breath to prevent choking on the dust, sprinted toward the house.

Sirens wailed, the police only moments behind them.

Beside her, Jeff stumbled as Stacy flung herself out from behind a tree and into his arms and sobbed. "Get Alex. You have to get Alex."

As Jeff set Stacy aside, Chelsea reached the front stoop first. With a sweaty palm, she twisted the knob and flung open the door. Ignoring the huge knot of fear churning in the pit of her stomach, she raced upstairs. *Let him be all right.*

Thoughts of Alex's smiling face peeking through the slats in his crib helped her overcome fatigue and loss of breath. Behind her, Jeff must have taken the steps four at a time to catch up so quickly.

They burst into the baby's room together. Her gaze flew to the crib.

Empty!

"Where is he?" she shrieked.

The window by the balcony was wide open. Suspecting the intruder had climbed through the window to leave, she raised her hand to stem her dizziness at the horrifying thought that he'd taken Alex with him.

*Don't faint. Alex needs you.* She gulped fresh air in the few seconds it took Jeff to search the room.

"Shh." He raised his finger to his lips.

A cooing noise came from below, and her heart pounded with hope. Together they rushed down the stairs, flinging open doors on the way. Jeff checked the bathroom. In two strides, he reached the tub and flung back the shower doors.

Alex lay in the bathtub, busily trying to pull his toe into his mouth. The baby's head turned toward them, and when he spied Chelsea, he grinned, those deep dimples on his face winking.

"Alex." Chelsea knelt and scooped him into her arms. His little warm body felt so good pressed to her. If anything bad had happened to him... She wouldn't think it. She breathed in his baby-powder scent and kissed his chubby, smooth cheek.

As she hugged the baby, Jeff put his arm over her shoulder and looked out the open bathroom window. "We should get out of the house. Just because the window's open doesn't mean the thief has left."

Stacy stumbled into the room, her eyes red from crying. "The police are combing the woods." Her gaze dropped to the baby. "Alex. Is he all—?"

"He's fine," Chelsea reassured her.

"I was so scared," Stacy muttered. "I wanted to come up and help him, but I made myself call the cops."

Jeff grabbed Stacy into a bear hug. "You did good. Real good."

Chelsea, grateful for the teen's quick thinking, had trouble keeping the trembling from her tone. If she'd panicked and run, Alex might not now be in her arms. "Thank you, Stacy. I only have one question."

"What?"

"Why was Alex lying in the bathtub?"

AFTER THE POLICE, who found nothing, made sure the house was safe, Chelsea packed, her hands still shaking.

Jeff returned to the room after a friend picked up Stacy and gave her a ride home. "I think we should head for the mountains."

Chelsea snapped shut her suitcase. "I'm going home."

He paced, his thighs tensing and releasing coiled energy. "You can't go home. It's not safe."

Chelsea sighed and sat on the bed. Her fingers played with the fringe of a pillow. "Until my memory returns, nowhere is safe. Perhaps it's time I stopped running. Then maybe my memories will return."

He stopped pacing directly in front of her and gripped her shoulders. "Did almost taking a bullet bring back your memory? Did almost losing Alex jar your mind into yielding its secrets?"

"But—"

"Did it?" he pressed.

"No."

"Someone is after you. Or Alex. You need to hide."

Her head jerked up and her eyes narrowed. "What do you mean, 'or Alex'?"

Like a volcano on the verge of erupting, he seemed barely able to control his anger. "What mere thief would stop and take a baby out of its crib? Think. There have been too many coincidences. Anne's murder, your accident at her house, being followed, a shot through the window at you. You have to face the fact that someone is after the baby."

The thought stunned her. "You think the thief was after Alex?"

Jeff paced again. His long legs ate up the room. "Why would a thief have touched the child? What's there to steal in a baby's room?"

"But if a kidnapper was after Alex, why didn't they take him?"

"Probably the arrival of the police. Running with a baby isn't easy, and the sirens could have scared the kidnapper into thinking he'd be caught if he'd been slowed by Alex in his arms. So he—or she—left Alex in the bathtub—a safe place, which means someone's been after the baby all this time."

The blood drained from her face, and she broke into a sweat. "You think Anne was murdered so someone could take her child?"

He spun on his heel and crossed his arms over his chest as if daring her to challenge him. "It makes sense. When you took custody of Alex, the murderer came after you. And when that failed, the murderer resorted to a kidnapping attempt."

"But who wants Alex?" Damn her lost memories. She raised her hands to throbbing temples. Why couldn't she remember?

"I don't know." A muscle in his jaw clenched, revealing his rage. "But the child has never been in danger. Only you."

"And Anne," she whispered. "I don't know. This makes no sense to me."

"I could be wrong. It's just a possibility that the baby is the target. But you and Alex cannot go home where you could easily be found." His voice dropped to a whisper. "I won't let you walk into danger."

Her chest squeezed tight. She couldn't risk Alex. If there was the merest chance that someone would try to take him, she would do whatever was necessary to keep him safe. Even if that something meant staying with Jeff until her heart broke into a thousand pieces.

She lifted her head and straightened her spine, suddenly anxious to be on her way. Somehow she would have to find the strength to keep an emotional distance between them. "So where are you taking us?"

"To my cabin in the mountains. It's a perfect place to hide—in a small town where strangers will be noticed. We can picnic by the lake, relax and let the police do their thing. I'll call my friend Garrick and have him watch the house while we're gone."

"You think the police will solve this any easier than Anne's murder?"

"What other choices do we have? Surely you don't want to hunt for Anne's murderer while carrying Alex in your arms?"

She held a bottle for Alex, and the baby sucked greedily, unperturbed by his encounter with the thief. Jeff was all too ready to take charge, make the decisions. And it would be so easy to just let him. She had to make herself argue. "And what makes you so sure that no one will follow us? If the town is isolated, we might be better off in a hotel in the city."

"I don't think so. A hotel is too public. It would be too easy to get to you or the baby there. You'd have to go out to eat. Maids and service people come in and out. A bribe might even secure a key to your room."

She leaned back, too weary to disagree again. She didn't want to fight with him and looked down from his piercing gaze. On her lap she held her appointment book. But as usual, the notations made no sense. The ominous word, "Obsession," underlined three times, still held no meaning. But the initials "C.O." reminded her that Carol Oxford should have returned this evening.

Picking up the phone, she dialed. "Carol Oxford, please."

After going through the switchboard, a cheery voice answered. "Hello."

"Carol, this is Chelsea Connors. Sorry to call so late—"

"What's wrong?"

How had the woman known something was wrong? "It's complicated. Could we drive out and talk to you?"

"We? You don't sound like yourself."

This woman obviously knew Chelsea well. There was no point in trying to fool her, and perhaps she could find answers to some of her questions. More importantly she might find out who was after the baby. "We'll drive out now, if that's okay."

Despite her exhaustion after making a slew of calls, Chelsea couldn't sleep during the ride to Old Point Comfort. Instead, she saw mental pictures of Anne and heard the haunting words of her nightmares. *Promise me.*

Chelsea still didn't know what those words meant. And she still hadn't found her missing gun. The police had searched pawnshops without coming up with a clue. Oddly the only good news these days was that Martin Tinsdale had agreed to run the firm until she returned.

THE IRON WAS POLISHED, the cord neatly folded and in place. The silverware was straight in the drawer. The dress shoes in the closet rested under dress suits, loafers under the casual clothes. The lint catcher from the dryer was scrubbed clean, and only a light dusting of the ceiling fans was needed before vacuuming the footprints from the rug on the way out the door.

*Perfect.* Everything was ready for the coming trip.

Chelsea and the doctor thought they were so smart. Finding out where they were going had been so easy. In their arrogance, they had become careless. And it would be their downfall.

THEY DROVE NORTH AND WEST, arriving in Old Point Comfort shortly before one in the morning. Despite the late hour, Jeff sensed Chelsea's keen anticipation. He only hoped Carol Oxford wouldn't disappoint her.

The sleepy tidewater village was home to fishermen, shipbuilders, yachtsmen and summer residents. Shuttered clapboard houses lined brick sidewalks. Petunias, hollyhocks and geraniums overflowed the gardens behind white picket fences. Surrounded on three sides by the bay, Oxford Inn crouched on the highest point in town like an old patriarch proud of family.

After Jeff parked, they entered a lobby of wood-pegged wall panels and hand-hewn oak beams.

A receptionist led them over rich burgundy carpet into a parlor with a giant fireplace that boasted a colonial heritage. On the walls of the cozy room were murals of nineteenth-century wallpaper depicting early-American scenes. The rear wall offered views of the Chesapeake, but Chelsea only had eyes for the tall woman who stood to greet them.

Carol Oxford's elegant attire, a long skirt and cream silk blouse with pearl earrings, matched the parlor's old-fashioned yet sophisticated decor. The two women locked gazes, and Carol reached around Alex to embrace Chelsea.

Chelsea stepped back and took Jeff's arm, her fingers gripping him so tightly he almost winced. "This is Dr. Jeffrey Kendall."

Carol looked him over from head to toe while he held her gaze. Finally she softened with what he hoped was approval.

"I've arranged for a late supper. You can rest and then tell me what's wrong." Her hazel eyes dropped to the baby. "Hi, Alex. You've grown since I saw you last."

"And when was that?" Chelsea asked.

Carol's head whipped up, and her eyes narrowed. "You know perfectly well I saw him when you drove Anne to her new home."

"I have amnesia." Chelsea said the words as if it cost her nothing, but Jeff felt her hand on his arm tremble. "I'm afraid I don't remember a thing. Not you, not Anne, nothing about my past."

"Amnesia?"

"It's a long story," Chelsea explained.

"Well, you all come sit down while I have Martha serve dinner. I'll do my best to fill in the details."

Carol Oxford had an innate kindness about her. She instinctively knew to pamper Chelsea without inundating her with questions. When they were seated around the table, Carol reached for Alex, and Chelsea handed the baby over to the woman without a qualm. She might not recognize Carol, but on some deeper level she instinctively trusted the woman.

Martha served them soup as if there was nothing unusual about dining after midnight. Jeff tasted the clam chowder and his brows rose. "This is terrific."

"Carol's a great cook," Chelsea said, dipping her bread into her bowl and taking a bite.

Jeff grinned. "Your memories are coming back."

"Just that one, I'm afraid." Chelsea turned to face Carol, her eyes apprehensive. "Are we friends?"

"Good ones. Anne, you and I roomed at Boston College together."

Jeff knew Chelsea must have a thousand questions about her past to ask, but her first thoughts were for Alex. "Do you know Alex's father?"

Carol's mouth quirked in a frown, and she sighed. "Anne would never tell us. She didn't want anyone to know."

"But why?" Jeff asked.

"Apparently she only dated the father a few times. And she was deathly afraid of him."

The blood drained from Chelsea's face. Jeff squeezed her shoulder. He didn't like the implications of Carol's words any more than Chelsea.

Carol's lips tightened in a grim line. "Anne never wanted Alex to know who his father was, so she never told anyone."

Jeff couldn't imagine a father murdering his son's mother. He felt so strongly that every child should have two parents that he'd decided never to marry, a responsibility he'd done his best to avoid.

But something had sparked within him when he and Chelsea had made love and shared warmth and need. And for the instant of a heartbeat, he'd had a desperate desire to believe in forever. Still, he'd felt guilty making love to her; he'd had to remind himself she was a grown woman and the choice had been hers.

Chelsea leaned forward, eager for an answer. "Why was Anne so afraid?"

Carol spoke with precision. "She described her lover as . . . 'compulsive.' That was her word for him. At first she was attracted to his good looks, his attention to detail, but when he started asking her to account to him for every minute of her day, she broke off their relationship. And he followed her."

Jeff finished his soup and pushed the bowl away. "Did she receive threatening phone calls?"

Carol's brows arched and her forehead creased. "I don't think so."

"Did she ever mention a gun to you?" Chelsea drummed her fingers and began to swing her foot.

"I believe he took her to a shooting range on one of their dates. Why?"

"There have been several attempts on my life. And I own a gun that is missing."

"You hate guns."

"I know. I think the man who murdered Anne is after me. Tonight someone tried to kidnap Alex."

Carol paled and her finger twisted in a tendril of her elegant updo. "You've got to leave here. Now."

Jeff heard the panic in the woman's voice and jumped to his feet. He strode quickly to the window and dimmed the light.

"I don't understand." Chelsea whispered.

"Anne was convinced Alex's father followed her here. I thought she was hysterical, but the next week, she was dead. If he knows we are friends, he could find you, too."

"YOU WEREN'T KIDDING when you said this cabin was out in the boonies." Chelsea grinned with the pleasure of almost feeling safe.

Just knowing she had a friend in Carol Oxford made her feel better about her past. Remembering Carol's cooking was a positive sign, and hopefully soon the rest of her memories would return. She tried to put aside the thought that a killer was stalking her in an attempt to kidnap Alex.

Western Maryland stretched into the Allegheny Mountains, and they drove past rolling farmland and apple orchards until the landscape turned to mountainous country sprinkled with azaleas, laurel and rhododendrons, which grew along the edges of the woods and scented the air with rich blossoms.

After driving across Maryland for most of the night, Jeff had swung off a side road onto a dirt path overgrown with grass and weeds, but their headlights showed a brush-free track that wound through woods of ash, birch, white oak and tupelo. Dawn started to break, but Jeff kept the headlights on since the thick foliage of towering oaks kept them in darkness. Chelsea rolled down her window and inhaled the sharp scent of evergreens and early-morning dew. Crickets and frogs chirped and croaked. A white-tailed deer fled from the path of headlights, deeper into the woods.

For the first time since they'd found Alex in the bathtub, the tension eased from her shoulders. Surely no one would find them out here. She looked behind her for the glow of following headlights—just in case.

Jeff reached over the sleeping baby and squeezed her hand. "I'd intended to head out to the cabin for my vacation, so I've had the place cleaned up."

She twisted in her seat to look at him in the dim light. He sat straight behind the wheel, and not an ounce of fatigue weighed down his voice. If she hadn't known he'd been up all night, she would have never guessed he must be reeling with exhaustion as she was. "Someone is expecting us?"

"Not exactly. I was supposed to be here yesterday."

"You delayed your vacation for me and never said a word?"

He shrugged and evaded a giant oak that the dirt track wound around. "I have a month off. A day or so lost is no big deal. And now that you're here to share the place, my vacation will be even better."

Alex picked that moment to awaken and started to cry.

"Oh, yes, Doctor. You'll get lots of peace and quiet on this vacation."

"I didn't come out here for peace and quiet."

She unstrapped the baby from the car seat. Jeff wasn't driving faster than five miles per hour, and ever since they'd passed through the private gate, there wasn't even the likelihood of meeting another car. "What did you come for?"

He wriggled his brows. "I thought I'd bring you out here all by yourself and play doctor."

Despite his teasing tone, heat flamed her cheeks. "You've already done that."

"This doctor likes to practice." He shot her a wry glance. "I've heard experience makes one more accomplished."

"Looking for compliments, are you?" She chuckled. "I assure you, the doctor seemed *very* experienced."

"Then the public-relations president was pleased enough to repeat the—?"

"If you're thinking of running a series of experiments with me, forget it."

"I could never forget you. The first taste of pleasure only whetted my appetite."

She absolutely could not make love with him again. The first time had been too soul shattering. If she allowed herself to become accustomed to such pleasure, she might never find the strength to walk away once Alex was again safe. And yet, up here in this romantic setting, how would she resist him?

She shouldn't kid herself. The setting had nothing to do with her wanting him. With the clean scent of his shampoo mixing with the male essence of him, she knew she wanted Jeff himself. His arms around her. His lips on hers.

She would never forget the moment he'd entered her body, his hands cupping her face, his eyes locking with hers. But more than the physical expression of love, she ached to repeat the intimate closeness of bonding. At that moment, she hadn't felt alone, but cherished like no other woman in the world.

The wooded area ended without warning. Ahead, like a topaz set in green velvet, lay the lake at dawn. From a cloudless sky, the sun sparkled over shimmering waters. A light breeze sent tiny ripples whipping across the surface, and several sailboards and one sailboat floated in the distance.

Her gaze took in a picturesque two-story stone mansion with sharp-slanting roofs and a massive fieldstone chimney overlooking the lake below. "That's a cabin?"

"Great-grandfather built it. My grandfather added on. Dad modernized it. And I enjoy it."

"It's yours?"

"I share it with my brothers and sisters."

They drove closer, and she noted wide wooden decks on the lake side. Floor-to-ceiling windows ran all the way to the A-frame roofline and took advantage of the spectacular view.

She shook her head, a grin on her lips. "And to think you had to ask me twice to come here."

"There's more. Down by the lake, there's a boat house."

"Perfect."

"We have a motor and sailboat, personal water vehicles and a sailboard."

"It's too bad we'll have to rough it," she bantered.

As he drove closer to the house, the breathtaking view held her mesmerized. "I don't see any power lines."

"Don't worry. We have a generator. Satellite television. Cellular phones. My sisters only liked camping at Holiday Inns, so over the years Dad added the modern comforts."

Jeff pulled up and parked beside the house. Chelsea got out of the car with Alex and stretched in the crisp dawn air. "Thank your sisters for me." She held the baby so he could see the lake. "Look, Alex. Have you ever seen anything so pretty?"

Jeff came up beside her and put his arm around her. His hand caressed the bare skin on her arm, sending a shiver of need straight to her weakened knees.

His tone was soft but harsh with pain. "It wasn't just a threat. You'd planned to leave me today, didn't you? If Alex wasn't in danger, you'd be back at your house, wouldn't you?"

A lump formed in her throat, and she turned away from him without answering, walked to the deck and sat on the porch swing. From a perfect perch, she rocked and watched the sun rise and spread peach-red fingers across the sky.

Jeff followed, took a seat next to her, but didn't touch her. "Tell me what you're thinking."

Like a dam bursting within, she let the words rush out. "I don't want a fling. I want forever. And despite the fact that I'm incomplete without my memories, I won't settle for less than marriage and children. I can't keep making love as if we have some sort of future. I can't lie to myself and pretend this will never end." She turned to him then, looked deep into his eyes and saw his pain. "Is that honest enough for you?"

He flinched but held her gaze. "I'm sorry. I never meant to hurt you."

This time she reached for his hand, and their fingers intertwined. It felt so right to her. Why couldn't he admit it? "I'll never regret one moment we've spent together. Without your help, Alex and I—"

"I love you." The words sounded as though ripped from the throat of a man dying of anguish. His face twisted in obvious pain. "But I have to let you go."

She leapt to her feet, suddenly furious. "Damn you, Jeffrey Kendall! How dare you tell me you love me but have to give me up to some highborn ideal. You can take your noble thoughts and shove them where the sun don't shine." Tears came to her eyes and her breath came in rasps, but she didn't stop shouting, not even at the shocked look on his face at her vulgar language or the fussiness of Alex in her arms. "Lie in your empty bed, night after night, alone, and choke on your nobility. And when you die an old and lonely man, you can regret that you could have had your precious medicine and me beside you, too, if you weren't so stubborn."

She clutched Alex closer and dashed toward the lake and the rocky beach by the shore. Jeff didn't follow. For that, she was grateful. She needed the time to regain her control.

The anger that had spewed from her lips had drained her. Exhaustion from last night's scare had her on edge. And Carol's information only added to the terror. Knowing Alex's father could be so cruel frightened her to the marrow. She sank to a large rock with the baby on her lap and welcomed the fresh breeze cooling her flushed face.

Alex reached for a pebble and tried to put it in his mouth. She gently pried it from his fingers and tossed it into the water. The baby seemed fascinated by the widening ripples, so she threw several more stones for him.

But her thoughts were on Jeff. How could she face him again after the nasty things she'd said?

And yet she didn't regret her eruption. Every word she'd said was heartfelt. After losing her memories, after almost losing her life, she'd found the courage to speak her mind. And yet her outburst had probably pushed him further away. Who was she to make demands on him? If she didn't love him so much, it would be easier to let go of the dream of waking up next to him every morning. But she wasn't one of those women who could hide her pain and let her man go on his merry way without fighting for what she wanted.

She sat by the lake for a long time. The gently lapping waters on the shore soothed her outward agitation. Nothing eased the ache in her heart.

This time by the lake with Jeff was simply an interlude in his life. She didn't doubt that he thought he loved her, but obviously it wasn't strong enough for him to want to keep her. More likely he'd confused lust for love.

And she had no business sitting here thinking about her future when someone was after Alex. She had to figure out who the kidnapper was before she lost the baby. But first Alex needed a diaper change, and she was ready to drop from exhaustion. When she returned to the house, Jeff was gone.

AFTER LEAVING Chelsea a note, Jeff walked through the woods, hands in his pockets, shoulders hunched and kicking clods of dirt. Every word she'd thrown at him stung like a dull hypodermic thrust to the bone. And he had no anesthesia against the pain, nothing to fight back with, since every word she'd spoken was truth.

Too anxious to hold his pace to a mere walk, he broke into a jog. But he couldn't run away from his churning thoughts. The fact remained that he wanted Chelsea Connors not for now, but always. Sometimes the desire to make love to her was so strong it was all he could do not to pick her up, carry her to bed and ravish her like some lusty pirate.

He couldn't marry her. He loved her too much to treat her the way his father had his mother. Yet giving her up would tear out a part of him he hadn't known existed.

He returned to the house an hour later, hot, sweaty and tired, with nothing resolved except the decision to make the most of their time together. Chelsea had taken Alex to one of the bedrooms, and Jeff headed for the shower.

He came out of the bedroom to the scent of fresh-brewed coffee and found Chelsea in the sunny kitchen, heating a bottle for Alex in the microwave. Plucking the baby out of the high chair, he whirled him around in a circle. "You like that, tiger?"

Alex broke into a huge smile.

"Oh, great." Chelsea shook her head but turned up her lips in a wry grin. "Twirl him around so he'll spit up all over me."

"I'll feed him." At the ding of the oven timer, he removed the bottle, pulled out a chair and rested Alex in the crook of his elbow. Right now fussing with the baby was easier than trying to make strained conversation with Chelsea.

She took a chair around the corner of the oak table. Her fingers fidgeted, and she crossed her legs, her foot swinging. "I want to apologize."

"No need. You spoke how you felt."

The room, except for Alex's sucking noises and the ticking of a clock, descended into another awkward silence. He risked a look at her, but she wouldn't meet his gaze.

"I'd say a change of topic is in order. How about a nap?"

"Maybe later. I'm too keyed up to sleep."

"Are you up for a picnic?"

She brushed the hair off her face, seemingly as ready as he to put her angry words behind. "I'd like that. I saw fresh groceries in the kitchen."

"I called ahead and had the caretaker clean and stock the place. There should be the makings of sandwiches in the fridge, maybe a bottle of wine. Mom keeps a basket and utensils in the kitchen, and there's a checkered blanket around here somewhere."

"I'll sling Alex in his knapsack carrier. How long will we be gone?"

"Ready for a hike?"

"Better make it a short one if we have to carry Alex and the picnic stuff, too."

"I want to take you to Dandy's Point. It's not far."

They seemed to have established a truce of sorts, each politely dancing around the argument that had come before. Jeff insisted on carrying the baby and the picnic basket too. The baby seemed content in the carrier that strapped him to Jeff's chest. His head was free to twist and turn, and his little fingers clutched Jeff's shirt.

By the time they passed through the dense woods and reached the small and intimate clearing on the hillside, he was holding Chelsea's hand, helping her over the rough spots. Their disagreement, although not forgotten, was firmly behind them.

"This is magnificent."

While she stood beside him enjoying the marvelous view of the leaves about to turn and the lake below, he took in her face, flushed pink from climbing the rocky peak. Although he didn't like heights and stayed well back from the edge, she didn't seem to notice that a step off the cliff could lead to a horrendous fall. She was breathing hard. Outlined against the sky, her chest rose and fell, drawing her sweater tight to the curve of her breasts, and he couldn't help recalling how she'd responded to him when they'd made love.

She'd given of herself without inhibitions. She'd given of herself generously and passionately. Cad that he was, he stirred at the sight of her windblown hair and proud neckline. If he had his druthers, he'd tear off her clothes and make love to her until her lips swelled from his kisses and she cried out his name.

Shoving his thoughts aside, he spread out the blanket and set to opening the wine. After popping the cork, he called to her. As if jerked out of her reverie, she spun toward him.

And a shot, fired from the wood, whizzed past Chelsea's head.

"Get down!" He lunged toward her, pulling her and Alex into the cover of the trees.

Alex started to cry.

"Hush, little guy. Shh." Jeff gently rocked the baby.

Although pale and with eyes wide, she ignored that she'd almost just died again and looked first to the baby's safety. With a smudge of dirt on her cheek and a scrape on her hand, she checked Alex, concern and fright in her eyes. "Is he hurt?"

"He's fine."

And then the thought that her life was again in danger struck her. He could see the horror in the darkening of her pupils, the trembling of her lip.

"The stalker found us." As realization at another close call set in, her entire body shook. She whispered, "How could anyone find us out here?"

"It could have been just a stray shot, some idiot out hunting." Jeff pulled her deeper into the woods. "But let's not take chances."

He'd been sure they hadn't been followed to the house. He'd diligently watched the rearview mirror. Only Chelsea's attorney, her secretary and Garrick knew where they were. Someone must have spilled the beans.

She swallowed hard, then looked right, left, back over her shoulder. "Right now I wish I had that damned *missing* gun. We're exposed out here. I feel like a target with a bull's-eye on my back. And if someone followed us, they know where we'll go back."

"Not necessarily. Are you up for a swim?"

"Alex isn't."

"I'll keep his head above water. Come on. I have the advantage of knowing my home turf. As a kid, I've explored every acre of this mountain."

To her credit, she didn't complain once but followed him, saving her breath for the difficult slides down the steep, rocky path. Alex, strapped firmly to his chest, barely slowed Jeff's movements or upset his balance, and he had his hands free to help Chelsea. Being busy kept the fear of heights at bay.

Above them something crashed through the woods.

They froze, and he pressed her into the side of the mountain, sheltering Alex and Chelsea as best he could from the clumps of dirt and pebbles raining down. Chelsea clung to him, curving her body over Alex. A protruding lip of rock above kept the small projectiles from reaching them.

A large animal, possibly human, crashed through the brush.

She shuddered. "What was that?"

"Could have been a deer."

"You don't believe that?"

He didn't answer. "Come on. The water's still cold this time of year, but it's only a twenty-five-yard swim to safety."

She took one look at the inlet that separated them from the boat house, turned around and bumped into him. "There's no way I'm letting you take Alex through—"

Another shot rang out, zinged across rock and echoed. It didn't hit near them, but her body jerked.

"I played water polo in college. We can do this."

"Swimming requires two hands. If Alex stays in that carrier, he'll drown."

Jeff unsnapped the baby, removed the diaper that would absorb water and weigh him down and debated whether to kick off his sneakers. "I'll swim sidestroke and keep his head above the water with my free hand."

"You want to risk Alex's life on the fact you once played water polo?"

"I'm still in shape." He cupped her chin with his hands and kissed her hard on the mouth. She tasted so sweet, so cold. Gently he pulled back. "Trust me."

As a third shot rang out, he kept his sneakers on and lunged into the water. He stifled a gasp at the coldness, grateful that the unusually warm summer had heated the mountain lake to an endurable temperature. Still, his muscles stiffened at the icy cold, and Jeff wouldn't have taken the baby in except under the direst circumstances. Oddly Alex didn't seem to mind the cold water. His eyes opened wide, and he gurgled happily.

Chelsea plopped in right next to him and let out a yelp. Thankfully she wasn't a bad swimmer. And the baby took to swimming like a duckling. He cooed and grinned, kicking his little legs.

Under other circumstances, a swim might have been fun.

Except when Jeff squinted up at the cliff, a shadowy figure pointed a glittering weapon at them.

# Chapter Eleven

Jeff scissor-kicked closer to Chelsea and placed his back between her and the danger on the cliff. Although she was a good swimmer, weighed down in clothes, it was slow going. Expecting a shot between the shoulder blades, he had to remind himself to take even breaths. Relief washed through him when they swam around the protective side of the boat house without mishap.

Dripping, they hurried to the house. Once inside, Jeff checked every room. Then, while Chelsea took Alex upstairs, Jeff locked the doors, checked the windows and drew assorted curtains, blinds and shades.

In the guest room, Chelsea stripped Alex of his wet clothes and tried to calm the pounding of her heart. "There, that's better. Now, after a warm bath, you'll be warm and cozy."

At the sound of a footstep, she turned to the door, her heart leaping into her throat. As a silhouette with a baseball bat in hand eased out of the dim hallway, she jumped and let out a gasp. When she recognized Jeff, she twisted her mouth in a sheepish grin.

He leaned the bat against the wall and handed her a towel. "Sorry. Didn't mean to scare you."

"It's okay. Did you call the cops?"

"Yeah. If you want to dry off, I'll hold Alex. I don't think we should leave the little guy alone for a second."

Until this moment, she'd been too busy surviving and caring for Alex to dwell on the thought they could have been killed. The surge of adrenaline that helped her slide down the cliff and swim was wearing off. The floor seemed to tilt beneath her. She swayed on her feet.

Jeff moved to her side and slipped his hand around her waist.

His eyes darkened with concern. "Hey, you're shaking. Relax." He wrapped the towel around her shoulders and drew her into his arms.

His heat chased away the chill. But no matter how much she wanted to lean on his strength, she was not about to allow him to pamper her and avoid talking about what had just happened—even if her suspicions clenched her stomach into a writhing coil.

"How can I relax when someone could shoot the lock off the door and get in here?"

Jeff picked up the bat. "I've called the police. They should be here soon. In the meantime, whoever is outside is probably gone."

She wanted to believe him. And the thought of a hot bath easing away the rest of her chill was damned appealing. But from the way he kept tapping the bat into his open palm, she suspected his words were more to reassure her than because he thought they were safe. He obviously didn't think those shots had been from a hunter any more than she did. Although she was going on gut instinct, he might have a good reason. "Why don't you think that shot was a hunter?"

"It's not hunting season. Plus I'm not positive, but I thought the gun sounded like a pistol, not a rifle. And..."

She leaned against his side, relying on his strength to guide her and Alex down the hall, drinking in his warmth to banish her chill. "And what?"

"I thought I saw a shadow on the cliff. Something metal glinted, and I could have sworn a pistol was pointed at you. But when I swam closer with Alex, the shot never came."

She stopped walking and shoved a dripping clump of hair from her eyes. "What are you saying?"

"I think that whoever fired the gun didn't want to risk hurting the baby. Carol may have been right. Your stalker, Anne's murderer, is Alex's father."

The peach fuzz on her arms stood on end. "Alex's father doesn't want to hurt his son—just me." Her voice rose in panic, and her teeth chattered. "Why didn't he just ask for visitation privileges?"

"Because he killed Anne. Remember the landlady said they had blood samples at the scene of Anne's murder? If Alex's father tried to claim him, he'd have to take a blood test. The minute he did, he'd be arrested."

Downstairs Jeff's portable telephone rang. He opened the bathroom door for her and then ran down the hall with the bat, his words coming from over his shoulder. "Run some hot water, and I'll be right back to help with Alex."

With trepidation that the phone call would only bring more bad news, she entered the bathroom and partially pulled back the red-and-black shower curtain, bending to turn on the hot water.

From over her shoulder, an arm shot out around her throat, crammed against her windpipe, cut off her air and yanked her back until her eyes focused on the gaping hole in the ceiling. Horror, biting and acrid, rose to clamp her chest in a vise.

She was going to be murdered just like Anne. Her life would be over, right here, right now. She struggled against the arm clamped around her neck. She fought back a wave of nausea. She was never going to make love to Jeff again, never going to see Alex grow up.

Poor baby. With her last strength, she clutched him to her chest.

A grating, whispered voice rasped in her ear. "Put the boy on the floor."

Realizing it was best to put Alex down before she dropped him, Chelsea did as she was told.

The pressure on her throat eased just enough for her to settle Alex on the rug. Then she was yanked backward against powerful, cruel strength. Her lungs ached, then burned.

*No, don't give in.*

With the last of her waning stamina, she dug back with an elbow. She failed to free herself.

She clutched the arm around her neck and strained downward in an attempt to draw breath. It was like trying to bend steel. She wasn't strong enough. Her lungs strained for air.

Willing herself not to give in to the encroaching darkness, she kicked vulnerable shins with her sneakers. Her attacker grunted but didn't release her.

By her feet, the baby cooed, his deep blue eyes staring into hers.

*Alex, baby, forgive me.*

Fire exploded in her chest. Her vision tunneled like a camera shutter flicking closed for the last time.

Dizziness turned to blackness.

JEFF REPLACED the receiver with a frown. The ringing had stopped just as he'd answered the phone. Hoping he hadn't missed an important call from the police, he took the phone with him back upstairs just in case they might call again.

Surprised not to hear the sounds of water raining down in the bath, Jeff went to see if Chelsea had delayed until he could take the baby. A wet, wriggling Alex could be quite the handful.

The absolute quiet sent the first prickle of alarm down his spine. Alex was often cooing, and Chelsea usually talked to the baby. Jeff didn't hear a sound.

Taking the last steps three at a time, he raced down the hall and skidded to a stop in front of the gaping bathroom door. An open ceiling panel revealed where the intruder had hidden. Chelsea, unnaturally still, lay on the cold tile floor. Jeff's knees almost buckled at the sight of her deadly pale face.

Dropping to his knees, he reached for a pulse, noted the strangulation bruises around her neck, simultaneously checked her breathing. Oh, God. Nothing.

He started CPR, never more thankful for his medical training than at that moment. Swiftly he calculated the time he'd been downstairs. It couldn't have been more than a minute. If he could revive her quickly, there would be little chance of brain damage.

Her heart started almost immediately, a good sign. And yet her lungs seems reluctant to respond. "Damn it, Chelsea. Fight. Come on, darling, you can do it. Breathe."

As his lips touched her cold ones and forced air into her lungs, fear he'd never known before socked him in the gut like a heavyweight's knockout punch. She'd come to mean too much to him to lose her. He wanted her. He needed her. He loved her.

And he wanted to spend the rest of his life with her. He wanted to give her children; he wanted to watch her grow old.

Why did it take an emergency before he'd admit the depth of his feeling for her? When she was with him, he could barely keep his gaze off her. He loved watching her laugh, he admired the courageous way she faced life and he'd never had another woman give so unstintingly of herself when they made love.

Her passion had inserted itself into the fiber of his life. Even when they weren't together, she was constantly in his thoughts. And the possibility of losing her now shot fear into his voice. "Breathe. Damn you, breathe. Alex needs you. I need you."

"WAKE UP. Damn it, Chelsea, wake up." Jeff called to her, and she forced open her lids. She was lying on the bathroom floor. Jeff knelt by her side, his face ashen. The worry lines radiating from the corners of his eyes had deepened, and his breath came in hard gasps.

"What happened?"

She fought the pain in her throat. "Choked. Where's Alex?"

He spoke softly while he checked her pupils. "When I found you, your heart had stopped. You weren't breathing. I had to give you CPR and mouth-to-mouth. I couldn't go after Alex and leave you to die."

Go after Alex? In confusion, she looked to the spot where she'd last seen him.

*No. God, no. Please let Alex be safe in his crib.*

She struggled to rise from the bathroom floor. Her chest hurt. Talking was pure misery but a minor discomfort compared to the agony burning inside her.

"Alex—?"

"He's gone. But I don't think his father will hurt him."

"No!" She wished she could sink back into the blackness. She pounded Jeff's chest with her fists. "No. I promised Anne. I promised—"

"Shh." Jeff ignored her feeble blows and drew her into his arms, pressed his cheek to hers while he rocked her against his chest. "We'll get him back. We'll find him."

She'd failed her best friend. She'd failed Alex. And she couldn't remember one thing Anne might have told her to help find Alex's father. Frustration and fear and rage surged through her.

If only she could remember. Surely Anne must have told her something that would help them now. But try as hard as she could, nothing returned, not one shred of a thought, not a phrase, not a mental picture.

She forced back a sob. "Did you see—?"

"No. Whoever took him was gone before I came back upstairs. How about you? Did you see anyone?"

"He came out of the ceiling, grabbed me from behind. He must have reached the house before we did."

Tears ran down her cheeks, and she angrily brushed them away with the back of her hand. "We've got to find Alex. Search the woods. Call the police. The FBI. The press."

"First you need to change out of these wet clothes and get into bed. The police will be here any minute."

"I'll change but I'm not resting."

He started to protest, then must have seen the blaze of anger in her eyes and decided not to argue.

THE LOCAL POLICE found nothing. After having Chelsea checked at the local hospital, Jeff and Chelsea stayed the night at the cabin and the next morning headed back to Chelsea's house. If the kidnapper intended to try for a ransom that was the likeliest place for him to call.

Despite Jeff's urging, Chelsea hadn't slept once the previous night. In turn she felt anger, outrage and emptiness. Deep in her heart, she knew Alex's father would not call and ask for a ransom. He'd pursued Alex with horrifying intent.

If they ever found Alex's father, they would also have found Anne's murderer. And the thought of her sweet, innocent baby in the hands of a murderer was enough to send her into tears. Except she had none left. She'd shed them all the night before, and not even Jeff's arms could comfort her.

On the long drive home, she'd slept fitfully.

Anne came to her in her dream. "Promise me. Promise you won't let anyone hurt Alex."

"I promise."

"And if something happens to me, you'll buy a gun?"

"Nothing's going to happen to you."

"You'll buy the gun, carry it with you to protect Alex?"

"Yes. Yes. I promise."

A horn blared and Chelsea awakened with a start. Her hand moved to the car seat. Alex wasn't there. For that first moment coming out of sleep, she'd forgotten. But then the numbing horror hit her with all the subtlety of a bulldozer. Alex was gone.

Jeff glanced over at her. "You were mumbling in your sleep."

"I promised Anne if anything happened to her, I'd buy a gun and use it to protect Alex."

Jeff glanced across the empty seat at her. "You remember that?"

"I dreamed it. But I know it happened."

"The dreams are probably your subconscious' way of prodding your conscious mind to remember. It's a good sign."

AFTER TWO STRAIGHT DAYS of waiting for the phone to ring, Chelsea had decided no one was going to call. Her nerves, frayed and tattered, jumped at the sound of Jeff coming up behind her in the den. The shot-out window, still boarded, and the bullet holes in the drywall were constant reminders of the violent man who had taken Alex.

"Why don't you go out for a while?"

She shook her head. Although the walls had closed in so that she found it hard to breathe and all she wanted to do was run until she dropped in exhaustion, she couldn't leave the phone. "Someone might call."

"I'll stay." He pressed his portable phone into her hand. "I'll call if there's any news. Go to the office and try and work. Maybe it will help take your mind off the endless waiting."

When she stepped out the front door, guilt stabbed Chelsea. She felt as though she was abandoning Jeff. And Alex. But she'd start screaming soon if she couldn't do something positive.

After what Carol had told her, she was sure Alex's father was the kidnapper, yet the police still checked every suspect. And had come up with nothing. The Carpenters supposedly hadn't left town. Their car was in the shop and it wasn't the gray Toyota that she remembered following her to the restaurant but a white Lincoln.

Martin Tinsdale had gone on a fishing trip with buddies over the weekend. When he'd returned, he hadn't had the baby with him.

The police had even questioned her copy editor, Vanessa, again, but she'd insisted she'd spent the weekend with her girlfriend. The cops were tracking down her story now, but Chelsea had no reason to suspect her.

Even Ms. Kilcuddy, the kindly lady from foster care, had come under suspicion. But of course, she knew nothing, either.

And no one could find Walter. Someone at her firm told the cops he often went deep-sea diving for the weekend. When he didn't show for work Monday morning, the police put an all-points-bulletin out for her accountant.

Damn. If only she could remember the man Anne had been running away from, it might lead her to Alex.

Jeff and she had torn the house apart from top to bottom in search of clues and ended up with nothing for their efforts. And yet maybe it was a leftover fragment from her dream, but something pulled at her memory, something she must have overlooked.

Chelsea walked into her office, and Sandy stopped polishing the arm of one of the antique chairs. "Have you heard anything?"

Chelsea swallowed hard. "Nothing yet."

Sandy wiped her hands on her skirt, her fire-engine-red manicured nails skimming her emerald skirt. "Would you like a cup of coffee?"

"No, thanks. If I put any more caffeine into my system, I'll be climbing the walls."

"Some herb tea, then?"

"That would be great." Now that she was here, Chelsea didn't know why she'd bothered to come in. She checked the batteries on the cell phone for the fourth time, willing it to ring.

But it was the office phone that rang. Sandy answered and handed her the receiver. "It's your attorney."

Her heart leapt. The newspaper had mentioned his name, and perhaps the kidnapper had contacted him.

"The Carpenters are dropping their custody suit," her attorney said.

Stunned, Chelsea wondered if they already had the baby. "What did they give for a reason?"

"They said they didn't want a flawed baby."

"There's nothing wrong with Alex."

"But he has the genes of a murderer. Totally unacceptable to the Carpenters."

Chelsea hung up not knowing whether to laugh or cry. Focusing on work was impossible. Flopping into a chair, she pulled her address book into her lap and flipped through the pages. Maybe the answer was there.

Many of the initials were now familiar to her. M.L. was Mark Lindstrom. W.B. was Walter Brund. C.O. was Carol Oxford. As she went through the entries from the past several months, her eyes focused on the word, "Obsession." For the hundredth time, she wondered what the entry meant.

"Here you go." Sandy handed her a cup of tea. "Is that nice doctor you brought to the Benedict party still around?"

"I don't know what I'd have done without him. Instead of taking his vacation, he's at my house, waiting to be contacted in case the kidnapper calls."

Sandy wiped imaginary dust from the desk. "And your memory?"

"I've started to dream about my past. Jeff says that's a good sign."

"Your voice changes when you talk about your doctor."

So her feelings about Jeff were that obvious? When Chelsea sipped her tea without commenting, Sandy continued. "I wish I could fall in love."

"Are you dating someone special?"

"I was." Her secretary hesitated as if debating whether to say more. Although they'd grown closer, they had not come to the point where they confided personal secrets.

"And?" Chelsea prodded, more to pass time than out of any real curiosity.

"At first I thought he was the greatest. He's easy on the eyes and treats a girl nice. Doesn't mind spending money on me, either. Then I started to notice little things that bothered me."

Chelsea no longer had to fake an interest. "What kind of things?"

"Well, you know how I like a clean office? I keep my house the same way. But this guy stops the car on the freeway to clean the windshield if a bug flies into it. Before he makes love, he folds his clothes. He's compulsive."

"Compulsive." Oh, God! *Compulsive* was the word Carol had used to describe Anne's boyfriend. Every nerve ending felt raw, and she could barely sit still. But surely Sandy and Anne couldn't have been dating the same man?

"And he told me he was single, not divorced. Yet this morning when I called, I heard a baby crying in the background. I think he's lying to me."

Chelsea dropped her teacup. There were too many coincidences for this to be an accident. Anne's killer had been keeping track of Chelsea through her secretary—that's how he'd found her at Jeff's cabin.

Had she been so obtuse not to pick up the fact that Sandy had been dating Walter? The police said Walter hadn't come back from his dive trip, but Sandy knew where he was.

Her voice trembled. "Sandy, where is Walter?"

Sandy's forehead furrowed. "I have no idea."

"But you said you called him this morning and heard a baby crying. I assumed—"

"I've been seeing Mark Lindstrom."

The name hit her like a sucker punch to the upper jaw. Her head reeled, but she was already running toward the door. She recalled Mark's fastidious military dress, his habit of cleaning his glasses with little square tissues, his taking Alex at the party. Everything fit.

And, once again, the word "Obsession" tugged at her memory.

"Mark's got Alex. He's been following me—using you to find me. Call Jeff and tell him to have the police meet me at Mark's place."

She skidded to a halt and looked back at her stunned secretary. Sandy's face had paled when she realized she'd been used. "I've been a fool."

"Count yourself lucky. I think Mark Lindstrom murdered Anne. Now, what's his address?"

## Chapter Twelve

When the phone rang, Jeff pounced on the receiver. But the kidnapper, not Sandy, was the person he'd hoped would call.

"Chelsea asked me to tell you that we think Mark Lindstrom has Alex."

"What?"

"We think Mark is the baby's father."

Sweat beaded his brow and trickled down his cheeks. The news pummeled him like a ten-pound sledgehammer pounding his head. "Where's Chelsea? I gave her the cell phone. Why didn't she call me?"

"She was in a hurry to find Mark. She asked me to call you and then have the police meet her at Mark's." Quickly Sandy gave him the address, an expensive part of town by the bay.

Jeff wrote it down, told Sandy to call Detective Burdett and then dialed his cell phone. *Come on. Pick up. Pick up. Pick up.*

"Your call cannot be completed at this time. The customer you dialed may have reached their destination or—"

Jeff slammed down the receiver. Surely she knew better than to single-handedly confront Anne's killer?

For Jeff, the trip to Mark's apartment was endless. He seemed to make no progress. All he could do was sit and wait for the traffic jam to clear.

And as if the traffic wasn't enough to delay him, the overcast skies suddenly opened. Slicing, needle-pointed bullets of rain shot at the windshield hard enough to puncture his heart and shatter his soul.

Guilt overwhelmed him. If he hadn't pressured her to go out, she wouldn't have been alone. In danger.

Trapped in traffic, Jeff leaned on the horn.

AH, EITHER CHELSEA had finally solved the puzzle or her memory had returned. Either way, Mark had prepared for this moment, welcomed a tidy resolution.

He replaced the phone, well-satisfied his C-note to the doorman had paid off. Opening the blind, he peered with his binoculars through the cleansing rain to the street below.

There she was by the fishing shed, her nose pinched tight against the smell. Such a filthy place. Her eyes, wide with fear, looked up as if to guess his position.

*Fool.* Although she'd evaded death, he'd stayed one step ahead of her.

And now he was ready to put his last plan into action. Moving to the kitchen, he wiped the counter and a smudge print on the toaster. The kid had messed up his schedule, to say nothing of the tidy bathroom, but all was back under control.

He lifted the soap sideways to balance on the edges of the container so the bottom of the bar wouldn't go soft. After straightening the dishcloth, he was ready to take on Chelsea Connors.

She'd interfered with his plans too many times to survive. And the doctor would be next. Then Carol Oxford.

Finally he and Alex would be alone, and the child would come to love him the way a son should. Anne had deserved to die for attempting to hide his son from him. And her friend Chelsea was no different.

Soon she'd be dead, too.

CHELSEA PULLED UP to a marina across the street from an elegant brick-and-granite apartment building. Mark's apartment. But from her parking spot, she couldn't keep the front entrance in sight. Despite the angry, dark storm clouds thundering overhead, she opened her car door against slapping-cold rain and stepped out. With her back to the gray Chesapeake churning with whitecaps, she scoured the busy apartment entrance and searched for a tall man in uniform and a baby.

Wind-driven rain matted her hair to her head within seconds of exiting her car. A rush of air whipped her jacket. She shivered but knew better than to approach the protection of the apartment building while she waited for the police.

Huddling in the three-sided, roofed shed where fishermen cleaned their catch, she counted the windows ten stories up and tried to ignore the fetid odor of rockfish, terrapin and hard crab. Tilting her head and shading the rain from her eyes, she wondered which apartment belonged to Mark Lindstrom.

When water trickled down her jacket and her neck cramped, she took in the busy street. Storefronts lowered storm shutters to protect the glass from flying objects. A French poodle barked. People huddled under newspapers, and the wind blew one poor woman's umbrella until it tore from her hands and tumbled across the apartment parking lot. She chased it, catching up only when the umbrella wedged against a gray Toyota.

From here, the Toyota's rental tag was plainly visible, and Chelsea's heart thundered. Mark had rented a car to follow her from work to where she'd met Jeff for dinner.

No wonder Anne had been taken in. Mark had fooled them all.

If she thought he would do the baby any harm, she would have been less patient. But she fretted over Mark's violent temper, which Anne had told her about. As she huddled from the wind and rain, shivering, Chelsea's memories returned. Not in bits and pieces, but as if a door unlocked in her mind to bid her entrance to the entire array of emotions, experiences, hopes and dreams.

Just as Carol said, Anne had never told either of them Mark's name. Anne hadn't wanted anyone ever to tell her son about his father, about what kind of monster Mark Lindstrom was or that she'd lived in terror of him finding her.

On the second date, Mark had raped Anne. Afterward he'd stalked her, telling her if she pressed charges he'd kill her.

Without telling Mark she'd become pregnant, Anne changed jobs, moved across the bay, had her baby. She'd thought she'd been safe.

But Mark had been clever, persistent, patient.

In the rain, chills shook Chelsea. Mark's cunning ruthlessness froze her to the bone. He'd waited for Anne to deliver Alex, then murdered her, probably not counting on Anne fighting back with enough strength to spill his blood.

Unable to come forward and claim the baby without taking a genetic test that would match the blood at Anne's house and tie him to the murder scene, he'd resorted to kidnapping. Chelsea recalled the distaste on Mark's face when Alex drooled on his uniform and prayed the insanely compulsive man wouldn't hurt an innocent baby.

Behind her, boats slammed against the dock, the halyards clanging against the sailboats' masts. The thunder and lightning had petered out, but the downpour never let up, and a deep fog rolled in. The foul odors of fish, stale gasoline and diesel fumes caused her stomach to clench.

Where were the cops?

She stepped from the protection of the fishing shed and gazed down the street, looking for Jeff. The cafés along the waterfront had lowered their awnings, their patrons moved inside.

Realizing she'd left the cell phone in the car, she walked toward it, keys in hand. She'd call the police herself.

A hard, metal object pressed into her side, and she dropped her keys on the pavement. A gun. Fear, pulsating and hard, drenched her in sweat. In contrast, her mouth went cottony dry.

"We're going for a nice boat ride," Mark Lindstrom growled into her ear. "You, me and Alex." Keeping the gun gouged into her rib, he spun her around.

The memory of Mark's gloating face right before he'd struck Chelsea's head at Anne's house caused her legs to weaken, her stomach to churn with nausea. He was the one responsible for her amnesia. He'd meant to kill her. Would have succeeded if not for the neighbor's dog.

With a cruel twist of her arm, Mark forced her onto the slick dock. He suddenly thrust a crying Alex into her arms. She clasped her baby to her breast, and his crying eased as he recognized her. Sheltering the baby under her jacket as best she could, she slid and slipped as Mark dragged her toward the marina.

"Where are you taking—?"

"Shut up."

She knew she should keep him talking, delay him until the police arrived. But when she opened her mouth, he jabbed the gun into her ribs so hard her knees buckled.

She lost a shoe and kicked off the other, hoping Jeff would find them, that Jeff would look for her. Mark paid no attention, dragging her barefoot through the pelting rain onto a floating dock that pitched and heaved with the waves.

Like in the fairy tale *Hansel and Gretel,* she wished to leave a trail—but of something more substantial than bread crumbs. Except the sea would wash away any item she dropped. The waves crashed over the dock, the seawater warm on her feet compared to the icy sluice of rain.

Bundled beneath her jacket, the baby made a warm spot against her chest. She hugged him tightly and wished she had the strength to jump with him into the sea. But even if she was willing to risk swimming with Alex the way Jeff had, Mark clutched her arm too tightly to break away.

He led her past boat slips filled with yachts, both power and sail, and several small dinghies.

"There." He pointed to a small rowboat. "Get in."

Horror coursed down her back. Surely he didn't mean to escape in such a small craft in the raging sea? She dragged her feet, but his brutal grip on her arm yanked her forward.

While he untied the bowline, she took off her watch, dropped it and used her toes to wedge it in the crack between two boards. She considered running. But there was no cover, only a straight path that would give him the easy target of her back. She took a good look at the weapon and recognized her gun—the one Anne made her promise to buy if anything violent happened, she noted painfully.

He pulled the boat closer and gestured with the gun. "Get in."

She stepped carefully into the bobbing boat. Not an easy feat while holding a baby. As soon as she sat, Mark nimbly jumped in and picked up his oars. In the distance, sirens wailed. But the police would cautiously search Mark's apartment building before even considering the dock. And until Jeff arrived, no one would know she was missing.

*Don't panic. Don't panic.*

She realized her voice might carry over the water. "Why are you doing—?"

Mark's eyes gleamed with an insane light. He tilted an oar to her head in an unmistakable threat.

She ceased talking. The slim chance of being heard above the storm wasn't worth being knocked out and of no use to Alex. Mark continued to row, his shoulder muscles bulging. Lord, where was he taking them? If he just wanted to kill her, he could easily do it now. The fact that he hadn't done so didn't reassure her. Knowing the way he'd stalked and planned Anne's murder, she suspected he wouldn't kill out of passion or rage but ruthlessly, cold-bloodedly, with a meticulously planned, foolproof scheme.

She didn't want to die. After losing and regaining her memory, she'd recalled her family, a mother in California with whom she hadn't spoken in over a year after some silly fight. Her father had died, but she had aunts and uncles and cousins. She had her love for Jeff. And she had a son.

No rotten SOB was going to take her life without a fight. But as the rowboat moved away from the dock and into the fog, hope seeped from her with every rolling gray wave that took her farther from land. If he planned to dump her overboard at sea and let the crabs feast on her flesh, it might be years before her bones washed ashore.

Jeff and her mother would never know what happened to her. Worse, little Alex would grow up with a maniac for a father.

Mark gritted his teeth against the rowing, his face flung up to the rain in glee. His lips smiled coolly as if he weren't about to kill her, but had asked to escort her for a ride in the park.

*He's enjoying my fear, the bastard.* Every time she shuddered, his lips turned up, his eyes brightened.

How well he had planned. Seeking her out for an advertising campaign through Classy Creations, keeping apprised of her whereabouts by dating her secretary.

Ahead the sound of the sea changed, stilling as if in the eye of a hurricane. The wind died a bit. And she raised her head and squinted through the fog.

They were on the protected side of a sailboat. Then the sailboat swirled into the wind, and the rowboat pulled up to the transom.

She heard an echo of Anne's voice as she read, across the rear of the boat in bold black letters, the boat's name.

*Obsession.*

# Chapter Thirteen

Jeff squealed to a stop in front of Mark's apartment complex, double-parking in the street. The police had already cordoned off the building. He'd spotted Chelsea's car, but when he couldn't find her in the crowd standing behind the barriers, bile rose in his throat.

Where was she? *Think.* She'd probably arrived before everyone else. Taken refuge out of the rain.

He spun in a circle to look for shelter and spied the fish shed near her car. Sprinting to the spot, he leapt over a puddle and glimpsed something shiny in the water. Halting, he turned and plucked keys from the puddle. But were they Chelsea's?

He tried the door of her car, and the click of the door lock sent a shudder through him. Grabbing the cell phone, he stuck it in his pocket and then turned back to look at the marina. Chelsea had dropped her keys halfway between her car and the shed. Had it been accidental?

He looked back at the apartment building. The police had positioned their SWAT team. They'd probably call Mark on the phone and try to talk him into releasing the baby. Jeff debated over telling the police that Chelsea could be inside, a hostage to a madman.

But the police wouldn't go in shooting, not with the baby's life at stake, and if Chelsea had tried to leave clues to her disappearance, every moment could count. Jeff forced himself to walk slowly, his gaze scanning the ground, the docks, the water.

A dark spot on the dock caught his eye. Blood?

Despite his plan to search carefully, he broke into a trot. And almost skidded over Chelsea's shoes. The choppy seas breaking over the dock forced him to slow his pace, but he didn't turn back. Five minutes later, he plucked her watch from between two boards.

Smart woman. She'd definitely left him a trail.

But now he was at a dead end.

Just a couple of rowboats bounced against the dock. Had Mark drowned her? He pushed away the devastating thought of her body lying under the gray sea.

If not to kill her, why would Mark bring her out here to a dead end? Because it wasn't a dead end.

With watch, shoe and keys in hand, Jeff raced back to the police. He found Detective Burdett conferring with someone from the SWAT team and rudely barged into their conversation. "After Chelsea found out Mark had kidnapped the baby, she came here. I found her keys in a puddle—" Jeff pointed "—and this shoe was farther down the dock. And her watch wedged between two planks."

"You think Lindstrom's got her?" Burdett asked. Without waiting for an answer, he radioed the coast guard and requested a small plane to search the bay.

Within minutes the coast guard radioed back that Mark Lindstrom kept a sailboat, *Obsession,* at the marina. But the fog would prevent a plane from spotting a vessel from the air. By water the coast guard would try to find the boat, but in this fog, with miles of coastline to search and hundreds of harbors in which to hide, they didn't have much hope until the weather cleared.

Jeff turned away before the cops could read the desperation in his eyes. He knew in his heart, if they waited until the weather cleared, Chelsea would be dead.

Returning to his car, he backed away from the crowd and drove toward the park. Praying Garrick was on duty at med-evac, he placed a call to his friend.

"I need a favor," Jeff explained after Garrick answered.

"You got it."

"It might get you fired," Jeff warned.

"No problem."

Five minutes later, Jeff stood in the middle of a clearing, waving his hands overhead as Garrick landed the helicopter. He ran beneath the whirling blades.

Garrick leaned across the passenger seat, shoved the door open and shouted, "You're pale as Casper the Ghost. I can take her up alone."

Jeff gritted his teeth and ignored his stomach turning itself inside out. He climbed into the plastic bubble and fought down the panic rising in the back of his throat.

"I'm ready to take—"

Garrick handed him a set of headphones with a microphone attachment. "You sure you're ready for a ride in this soup?" The words came through the headset clearly.

Jeff yanked his seat belt tight and clenched his thighs with his fingers to keep them from shaking. "Let's go."

"Hell of a day to conquer your fear of heights." Garrick's grin contradicted his words. "Where to?"

"He's got a boat called the *Obsession* that's probably no longer anchored at the marina."

The helicopter rose, and Jeff's stomach lurched. Garrick's hands and feet constantly adjusted pedals, hand controls and dials. A sharp gust battered the chopper, but then he regained control with a burst of speed and veered toward the coast.

"I'm going to have to take her in low. There's a pair of binoculars under the seat."

Jeff tried to keep his head steady on the horizon while he grabbed the binoculars and opened the case. "Sailboats have a top speed of what?"

"Ten knots. How long's she been gone?"

"Not more than half an hour."

"So we'll search within a five-mile radius of the marina." Garrick glanced at Jeff. "What are we going to do when we find her?"

Fighting nausea, Jeff found bottled water under his seat and took a swig. "Trail them and call in their location to the coast guard."

Garrick shook his head, started to say something. Wind and rain buffeted the bubblelike craft. Jeff's nails dug desperately into his thighs. And they swooped, fishtailing and skidding through air like a skater across ice. After another steep dive, the chopper clawed upward, and his teeth clenched until the cords in his neck ached.

While the helicopter's unpredictable movements frightened him, Garrick appeared to enjoy the challenge. "Nothing to worry about. She's just bucking the wind."

*Nothing to worry about, my ass.* Garrick could lose his license for this little stunt. Hell. They could both lose their lives.

But he wasn't about to let the woman he loved face a murderer alone. He didn't want to lose her.

He brooded over it as the chopper swept back and forth in some kind of crazy pattern. Then out of the mist, a white cigar-shaped object appeared.

"Is that her?"

Jeff raised the binoculars to his eyes. *Obsession* was written in bold black letters across the rear. His gaze shifted to the cockpit. Chelsea huddled with the baby in a corner. The bastard hadn't even let her go below to the cabin to get out of the rain.

Mark reached into his jacket.

"He's got a gun!" Jeff yelled, expecting Garrick to pull the aircraft up. The chopper dropped lower.

Garrick threw a sling into his lap. "I'll lower you onto the boat."

Below, Chelsea screamed and Jeff made up his mind.

WHEN CHELSEA LOOKED UP and spied Jeff in the helicopter, adrenaline and renewed hope surged through her cold bones. If Jeff could master his fear of heights to rescue her, the least she could do was help.

With Mark distracted, Chelsea maneuvered Alex into the bottom of the cockpit where he couldn't fall. Pulling an oar from the deck where Mark had stored it, she almost had the paddle in striking position when Mark noticed her antics.

She swung the oar hard, but instead of hitting his head or knocking him overboard, she whacked the gun into the sea.

Mark roared in pain at the damage to his hand. He let go of the tiller and started to come at her, murder glinting razor sharp in his eyes.

She reached for Alex. "Don't step on the baby!"

"He's mine."

The boat pitched, Alex rolled, and she scooped him into her arms. "The tiller!"

In his haste to murder her, Mark had released the tiller. The sailboat broached in the heavy seas. The next wave flipped them upside down.

Pitched into the sea, Chelsea closed her arms around Alex. Stinging seawater washed in her eyes, her mouth, weighed down her clothes. Kicking with all her might and with lungs straining, she swam toward the surface and Jeff.

Jeff, who had come for her. The thought warmed her heart, gave her strength, pushed her on long after she'd exhausted her last reserves of energy.

Her head broke the surface, and she gasped for air. She raised Alex's head out of the water. He choked, then grinned.

Then Jeff was there, swinging from a harness, and she handed the baby to him. "He's choking."

Jeff gave her a thumbs-up and started to check Alex while the lift took him and the baby skyward. Chelsea treaded water and tried to calculate how long she'd been under. It couldn't have been more than a few seconds, but she worried that Alex could have breathed water into his lungs and tried to console herself Jeff would know what to do for the baby.

It seemed an eternity until Jeff descended again. From the smile on his face, she knew Alex was fine.

She barely had time to smile in return before a hand clenched her ankle, dragged her under. Mark!

Jeff splashed into the water beside her. He and Mark struggled over her ankle. Chelsea kicked hard and freed herself to pop to the surface. Flinging back her hair, she spied Jeff right beside her. Gently he brushed her wet bangs out of her eyes. "It's going to be okay. The baby's fine."

"Mark?"

Jeff swam closer. "He didn't make it. I tried to save him, but he fought me. I don't think he could swim."

Relief that Mark could no longer threaten her lifted like a two-ton weight from her shoulders. And then she felt guilty for her uncharitable thought. Reminding herself that he'd brought his fate on himself and it wasn't her fault Mark had died made her feel marginally better.

Jeff must have guessed at her conflicting emotions. He tilted her chin and kissed her. "I love you."

As his lips touched hers, she shoved thoughts of Mark firmly behind. "Oh, really? And just when are you going to prove you love me?" she teased.

"I jumped out of a helicopter for you. What more do you want?"

"Marry me, Jeff."

"Hey, the guy's supposed to do the asking."

"So ask."

"I'm afraid of rejection."

"Ask me, damn you."

"I'm supposed to do that on my knees, not while treading water."

She chuckled. "I can think of better things for you to do on your knees."

"Make an honest man out of me?"

She threw her arms around his neck. "Yes. Yes. Yes."

They kissed underwater and when they surfaced, he put her into the harness. As the winch took her up, he yelled, "Remind Garrick to come back for me."

"What?"

He shouted but she couldn't hear him. She was too close to the roar of the helicopter. But as soon as she climbed in and gathered Alex into her arms, she realized there was no room for a third person.

Despite the fact she knew Jeff was a strong swimmer, tears streamed down her cheeks. When Garrick returned, he might not be able to find Jeff.

"I'm going to set you down in the park. It's the closest place." Garrick tossed car keys into her lap. "Jeff's car is parked there. "Get the baby warm. I'll be back in a few minutes."

Those few minutes seemed a lifetime. She checked the clock on the dash, then checked it again. It hadn't stopped; it just kept time in slow motion while her heart raced. If she hadn't had Alex to fuss over, she might have bitten her nails to the quick. And then she heard the murmur of the helicopter returning.

And Jeff opened the car door and slid inside. "I decided on a career change."

"What?" She expected a kiss, a hug, an I-was-worried-about-you, so-glad-you're-safe comment. She hadn't even had a chance to tell him she'd regained her memories, including the link she'd recalled between Anne and the word "Obsession."

She took a deep breath and focused her thoughts on Jeff. When he'd proposed, she hadn't had time to think things through. But she didn't expect him to make such a sacrifice for her. "I don't want you to give up medicine for me."

"I'm not."

Had he changed his mind about marrying her? His words had her thoroughly confused.

He took off his shirt and tossed it on the floorboard, and she had to force her gaze away from the magnificent golden skin of his chest to eyes sparkling with excitement. "I'm going to specialize in pediatrics."

She still didn't understand. "But—"

"I'll go into practice with four or five other pediatricians. I'll only be on call one or two nights a week. Don't you see? The demand on my time and the number of emergencies will be lessened to give me more time to spend with my wife and kids."

Stunned by his decision, she felt her pulse pound, flooding her heart with happiness. He was so good with Alex, he'd be a wonderful pediatrician. "Are you sure?"

His fingers cupped the curve of her chin. His thumb teased her lips, cutting off her protest. "It's what I want for us. I asked Garrick to be my best man at our wedding. That okay by you?"

She was going to burst if he didn't kiss her. His male heat scorching her, she leaned over the baby and kissed him, melted into him. "Everything's okay with me, now that I have you and Alex."

## HARLEQUIN®

# INTRIGUE®

## COMING NEXT MONTH

**#381 RULE BREAKER by Cassie Miles**
*Lawman*
Aviator Joe Rivers was hell-bent on discovering the real cause for
his wife's fiery death in a plane crash. But he didn't expect to find
himself falling in love again—and with a prime suspect. After all, it
was sexy Bailey Fielding who helped pilot the craft in which Joe's
wife was killed....

**#382 SEE ME IN YOUR DREAMS by Patricia Rosemoor**
*The McKenna Legacy*
Keelin McKenna dreamed through other people's eyes...victims'
eyes. And when Keelin came to America in the hope of reuniting the
McKenna clan, the dreams intensified. This time she couldn't ignore
them—because somewhere out there was a father whose teenage
daughter was missing. Tyler Leighton would come to rely on Keelin
much more than she ever dreamed possible.

**#383 EDEN'S BABY by Adrianne Lee**
In the past, a woman had killed for Dr. David Coulter's love. Now
the lovely Eden Prescott has pledged her love to David. But when
she discovers her pregnancy, should Eden turn to the father of her
baby...or will that make them all—her, David and the coming
child—mere pawns in the game of a jealous stalker?

**#384 MAN OF THE MIDNIGHT SUN by Jean Barrett**
*Mail Order Brides*
Married to a stranger.... They're mail-order mates, and neither one is
who they claim to be. Cold Alaskan nights roused a man's lust for a
warm woman—and Cathryn matched Ben's every desire. He would
enjoy sweet-talking her into divulging her deepest secrets...for she
had slipped right into the ready-made role he had planned for her.
And right into the trap he'd set....

## AVAILABLE THIS MONTH:

**#377 CISCO'S WOMAN**
Aimée Thurlo

**#378 A BABY TO LOVE**
Susan Kearney

**#379 PASSION IN THE FIRST DEGREE**
Carla Cassidy

**#380 DREAM MAKER**
Charlotte Douglas

Look for us on-line at: http://www.romance.net

# HARLEQUIN®

# I N T R I G U E®

## What if...

You'd agreed to marry a man you'd never met before,
in a town you'd never been, while surrounded by
wedding guests you'd never seen before?

### And what if...

You weren't sure you could trust the man
to whom you'd given your hand?

### Don't miss

#384 MAN OF THE MIDNIGHT SUN
by Jean Barrett
August 1996

Where mail-order marriages
lead newlyweds into the mystery
and romance of a lifetime!

Look us up on-line at: http://www.romance.net

MAILO

## HARLEQUIN®

# INTRIGUE®

> *To my darling grandchildren,*
> *I leave you my love and more. Within thirty-three*
> *days of your thirty-third birthday you will have in*
> *your grasp a legacy of which your dreams are made.*
> *Dreams are not always tangible things, but more*
> *often are born in the heart. Act selflessly in another's*
> *behalf, and my legacy shall be yours.*
>                                    *Your loving grandmother,*
>                                    *Moira McKenna*

You are cordially invited to the McKenna Family
Reunion! Share in the legacy of a lifetime
as only Patricia Rosemoor—and
Harlequin Intrigue —can deliver.

The McKenna clan—some are good, some are evil.... If
the good prevail, there will be a family reunion. Find out
in the exciting McKenna Legacy trilogy:

#382 SEE ME IN YOUR DREAMS
#386 TELL ME NO LIES
#390 TOUCH ME IN THE DARK

Coming in August, September and October from
Patricia Rosemoor and Harlequin Intrigue.
Don't miss any of them!

HARLEQUIN®

# I N T R I G U E®

# WANTED
## 12 SEXY LAWMEN

They're rugged, they're strong and they're WANTED!
Whether sheriff, undercover cop or officer of the court,
these men are trained to keep the peace, to uphold the
law...but what happens when they meet the one woman
who gets to know the real man behind the badge?

Twelve LAWMEN are on the loose—and only
Harlequin Intrigue has them! Meet one every month.
Your next adventure begins with—**Joe Rivers**

in
#381 RULE BREAKER
by Cassie Miles
August 1996

# LAWMAN:
There's nothing sexier than
the strong arms of the law!

Look us up on-line at: http://www.romance.net

LAWMA

BRIDE'S BAY RESORT

# UNLOCK THE DOOR TO GREAT ROMANCE AT BRIDE'S BAY RESORT

Join Harlequin's new across-the-lines series, set in an exclusive hotel on an island off the coast of South Carolina.

Seven of your favorite authors will bring you exciting stories about fascinating heroes and heroines discovering love at Bride's Bay Resort.

Look for these fabulous stories coming to a store near you beginning in January 1996.

**Harlequin American Romance #613 in January**
*Matchmaking Baby* by Cathy Gillen Thacker

**Harlequin Presents #1794 in February**
*Indiscretions* by Robyn Donald

**Harlequin Intrigue #362 in March**
*Love and Lies* by Dawn Stewardson

**Harlequin Romance #3404 in April**
*Make Believe Engagement* by Day Leclaire

**Harlequin Temptation #588 in May**
*Stranger in the Night* by Roseanne Williams

**Harlequin Superromance #695 in June**
*Married to a Stranger* by Connie Bennett

**Harlequin Historicals #324 in July**
*Dulcie's Gift* by Ruth Langan

Visit Bride's Bay Resort each month wherever Harlequin books are sold.

HARLEQUIN ®

BBAYG

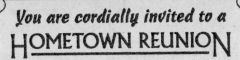
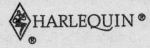

**Sabrina    It Happened One Night**
**Working Girl    Pretty Woman**
**While You Were Sleeping**

If you adore romantic comedies then have
we got the books for you!

Beginning in **August 1996** head to your
favorite retail outlet for
**LOVE & LAUGHTER**™,
a brand-new series with two books every
month capturing the lighter side of love.

You'll enjoy humorous love stories by favorite
authors and brand-new writers, including
JoAnn Ross, Lori Copeland, Jennifer Crusie,
Kasey Michaels, and many more!

As an added bonus—with the retail purchase,
of two new Love & Laughter books you can
receive a **free** copy of our fabulous
Love and Laughter collector's edition.

**LOVE & LAUGHTER**™—a natural
combination...always
romantic...always entertaining

 **HARLEQUIN** ®

Look us up on-line at: http://www.romance.net